KNIGHT JUSTICE

JC ERNST

Copyright © 2016 JC Ernst
All rights reserved.

ISBN: 1530372437
ISBN 13: 9781530372430

To my grandchildren: No grandparent could be more blessed and inspired than I.

Special thanks to Cynthia for the ideas and encouragement as we traveled along this path.

PROLOGUE

JANUARY 9, 2001.
ALEXANDRIA VIRGINIA

I staggered out of the bedroom wiping the small sand-like granules from my puffy eyes. The day to day routine and rigor had already caused my legs to feel like stumps and my brain to work in slow motion. Fortunately, I was nearing the end of my formal training and I had already been packing up my small apartment. I was to ship the things I wanted to keep back to Seattle. That was the easy part. Getting back to Seattle all in one piece was a whole different story; a story that could not be told on an empty stomach.

"Food and coffee that's what I need." I muttered as I wandered over to the cupboard and grabbed the first box of cereal I saw. Yes, Kellogg's Frosted Flakes was my first, every morning choice.

It's not the sugar that I am drawn to, it's the crunch. This was a regular part of my morning rationalization.

As my eyes began to clear, I noticed the Seattle Star lying on the kitchen table. I barely remembered dropping it there the night before as I trudged off to bed. I began to leaf through the pages of the news. I read on the second page: hostage demand, ten million-dollars.

"She's worth more than that," I said to myself as I reached for that first cup of Java.

I resisted the urge to pick up the paper and consume the details. My priority now was my grumbling stomach. Yet, I continued to search the paper for information.

Glancing back at the newspaper, I fumbled for and grasped the refrigerator door. As I read on, the door swung open. Managing only a clumsy grip, I secured the milk in my left hand and poured the white liquid straight into the bowl I had taken out of the dingy cabinet. With my neck now careened to the side, I scanned the article in order to find more details regarding the ten million dollar ransom proposed for Sherry Paul. Sherry was the agent I had put in harm's way and the very reason I was in this mess in the first place. The good news was she was alive! At least that's the way that I looked at it at the time. The paper this morning was really no different than other mornings except, now, there was a hostage ransom demand and she was still my responsibility.

I reviewed the other articles carefully posted on the paint peeled wall next to the old white GE refrigerator. There were six. As I leaned from side to side, chomping at my cereal, I read through the article papered wall, for the umpteenth time. The news stories renewed my frustration, anxiety and frankly, my anger. Today my heart was pounding stronger and in a much more menacing way than ever before. My hands were shaking. I guess the evidence that Sherry was, in fact, a pawn for trade, sickened me and I had a gnawing in my stomach as if a new and even more powerful punch had just been delivered to my midsection. Somehow the hope found in my stronger faith could not erase the impact of the news.

The first article was so familiar that if required, I could recall it verbatim. It provided details on the capture of the two thugs, Carlos

Castilano and Hadamid Zucara. These two were the supposed masterminds of the kidnapping and school caper. Masterminds ha, they were just two bit players.

The second article described in detail the story of the chip found within the computer at Cedarvale High School. It was not clear how much if any money had been diverted from the network of school computers. What was clear is that the chip was not supposed to be there. The article also outlined the facts surrounding the apparent kidnapping of a staff member, Sally Scantz. She was actually named Sherry Paul. She had been under cover at Cedarvale High school. I had been the Principal. The third and fourth articles described the intrigue surrounding the upcoming Castilano and Zucara hearings and possible trial.

The fifth and sixth were opinion pieces. I have to admit they outlined fairly accurately the "desertion of my post" as the principal of Cedarvale High School. The sixth article made brief mention of the rouse made by Sherry Paul who had "apparently" been "masquerading" as Sally Scantz a teacher at Cedarvale.

Now as I read this seventh article, I was not surprised to find that the teacher Kareem Razier had disappeared at the same time as Sherry Paul. This was during the mass disruption of the School assembly. The article questioned whether or not Razier was a hostage too. I had my own belief that he was not, in fact, a hostage and most of my buddies felt the same. Of course, I was well familiar with all the material because I had lived through the nightmare along with Sherry, who did masquerade as a teacher. She volunteered in an attempt to foil the terrorist plot. Which in some ways, I guess she did, if the articles could be believed.

I was living this growing disaster. I was doing a fast track agent development program assisted by Christian D. Poincy a long time mentor and friend of Sherry. I only knew of him through Sherry. She assured me that he was a trustworthy person and on that recommendation I risked it all.

I was training with people I did not know well. I had decided to join this secret underground organization I did not yet trust and ironically the only reason I was there was Sherry. She had, coaxed me into this bizarre experience. I had known her for years but college took us in different directions. Eventually I met and married, had children and on our way to happy ever after my wife died from cancer.

I was told that I would be part of the rescue attempt on Sherry, if she was still alive; when I was ready. I would also have to be accepted by the Knights. In the meantime, I would have to be prepared as a witness as I had been subpoenaed to testify. At the same time I was learning to be an underground activist. As they say in the Order of the Knights of St. John, invest in your adventure.

Invest I did, and in a big way. I left my job and my two kids, for what to my family must have seemed a fool's mission. Anyway I guess I should back up for a moment I am getting ahead of myself.

CHAPTER 1

November 11, 2000, Knightmare Begins

It was a normal November day in Seattle. The mist had already created small puddles on the cool damp blacktop. The cold air and low hanging fog only added to the frustration and sense of loss I was feeling. I was in on the plan from the beginning. Sherry was to serve as bait and I was to sit back and watch it happen. As you might imagine, I wasn't too happy with my role and was less excited about Sherry's. I have to admit that I was sold on the project before I was ready to make a good decision. So much for my impetuous nature, something about me I often must relearn.

I am pretty sure if you would ask if I made a good decision I would have to say no. But that is all behind us now. We had been told by the hot shot, Ieke Rollands, a retired Army Major General that Sherry was in very little danger. The Rangers, Ieke's buddies, had been recruited specifically to prevent Razier from taking her. One of them, the hulk like army ranger known as AJ, was the insurance plan. At least that's what Ieke led us to believe.

1

Like me, AJ felt his stomach grab onto his windpipe as he watched the van swerve. It just missed a green Acura CL. The GMC lurched and nearly rolled over as it left the school lot behind the gymnasium. AJ ran a few yards as he watched the dirty white rig turn left. He heard the tires screech as it angled up the hill disappearing from sight. He couldn't possibly see what was beginning to happen within the speeding van. AJ didn't know that there was a traitor inside. He raised then lowered his gun, yelled and kicked at the ground as he realized he had risked life and limb for nothing.

⋏

Sherry Paul, a strikingly beautiful brunette teacher was not supposed to be taken. She was the only pawn in the big gambit. She was going to be the hero in the capture of the internet thieves. At least that is what most of us thought. For Sherry, the effects of the chloroform and errant tazor shot were slowly subsiding. Moments earlier she had been whisked out of a school assembly. She had been rendered senseless and that's why she was so easily captured. She had been tossed like a bag of garbage onto the floor of the vehicle as it sped away.

Inside, she was beginning to mumble. Nobody was listening. She squinted through her now foggy green eyes and identified Kareem Razier. She knew him as the dark-haired, tall, cocky teacher colleague. She could also see the back of the head of the Islamic fundamentalist. He had been playing a role as a student in her school, the very same school where she and Razier taught; the school where I was principal.

She thought she could see the driver, the masquerading student Cazided. He seemed to be struggling with the army ranger in the van. The army ranger, a life hardened tough guy, was wearing green army fatigues. He was supposed to be one of the good guys. That is what she had been told. That is not how things happened. Still rolling forward, the truck was bouncing to and fro. As it did, Sherry was thrown from one side to the other.

The delivery van was now bounding through a patch of woods on what was no more than a cow trail on the back side of an old farm east of Seattle. The vehicle became airborne and landed hard as it headed down a steep incline. In her semiconscious state, she could tell the driver was losing the battle. The Ranger was part of the backup plan. Unfortunately for her, there was no backup plan. At least her safety was not part of any plan.

It was as if she was dreaming. She saw the images of legs crashing against her own but she could not feel the pain. A large, well-muscled arm pressed against her face and moved down to her chest. As the arm moved across her chest, she saw what she thought was the image of an x suspended above a crescent in blue ink on the forearm of the guy in the fatigues. The van suddenly slid sideways to a stop. An instant later, the side door slammed open. Sherry, still stunned, could feel the burn on her tongue and smell the foul odor. Her eyes burned as the van filled with a stinky white fog. She restrained the gag reflex as her eyes lost the ability to focus. Sherry could not feel Razier drag her to safety. The truck was now totally filled with a milky fog.

She fought hard to stay awake. Sherry again began to feel the tingles that signaled the loss of feeling in her long athletic legs; muscles honed from years of running 10 K races. She had felt the numbness before but only after climbing steep hills at the end of an uphill sprint. This was the first time she was feeling the effects of a nerve numbing gas. She heard a voice she could not see. She barely felt her arms and yet her log like legs, still stung as they banged against tree stumps protruding from the marshy ground. Then Sherry heard a roar as the van splashed into the water.

Razier glanced over his shoulder as he felt the percussion of the partially airborne auto breach into the swamp not more than 20 feet away. He could still see the now motionless Cazided, imprisoned in the four wheeled casket. Razier shook his head slowly in disbelief: Cazided was to be helping out with the capture of Sherry. Instead, Cazided was being murdered right in front of him.

The murderer joked as he watched the rig slowly slip into the murky brown water, "anchors away me lad."

Razier blinked a couple of times. He was confused as he considered the last few bubbles escaping from the slimy watery grave. Now he was a party to a murder. Not something with which he was prepared to deal. He was not told about this new role, nor was he happy to see Cazided gone. It was just one of those unknowns that he would have to adapt to. He had been willing to participate in the theft of the passwords from the school computer. He didn't even mind when he had been ordered to supervise the kidnapping. However, murder was not what he had envisioned.

The second man, the man with the tattoo; the traitor, the man who momentarily released Sherry's arm, was now quickly pulling the fatigues from his chest and legs. He simply stuffed the t-shirt in the pants. He put a large rock in the pocket and tossed them into the swamp. His grotesque smile stretched across his red and puffy cheeks as he and Razier watched the fatigues slowly slip into the murky water of Beaver Pond.

The clothing was now following the last and only occupant of the sinking van. The tattooed man was the killer. The fake student, Cazided was again a figment, just as the big man, the man with the money, the man with the ideas had planned and directed. Razier was in much deeper than he wanted to be.

Simultaneously, Sherry lay quietly on the ground as she struggled to gain back clarity, not fully aware of what had just transpired.

Was she dreaming or was Kareem Razier there? Just moments earlier he had been her colleague. Yes, she already believed Razier to be one of the bad guys, but she was not sure. *It can't be, they couldn't have, or did they? Did Razier and an army ranger save me from the sunken van? I'm so confused,* she thought as she reran the scene through her foggy brain.

Steeled by years of discipline and exhaustive training, she was motionless and seemingly out of it. All the while her normally computer like brain was now screaming for an upgrade. She was attempting to catalog and compile streams of data. Now she was just like the computer system these guys messed up. Just one little chip had the capacity to foul up a million computers nationwide. She was one of a handful of people that were trusted with a job. Her mission was to protect the national educational system from the attack. She wanted answers but she had no way of knowing whether she had been successful.

She did not compute or know exactly what was really happening. It was as if her head was floating above and away from her body. She had been gassed. Razier and the other guy were yelling but she was unable to figure out the context of the conversation. She felt little and understood less.

"You animal," Razier yelled, "I saw you trying to grope her. Keep your hands off or you'll get nothing out of this. I don't care who brought you in on the scheme."

The tattooed guy just laughed in a loud and guttural way. It was as if he wanted to remind Razier that he was the alpha ape and the deeper and stronger his noise the less he would be questioned.

Moments later Sherry's short rest in the woods was interrupted. As she was again being dragged: she barely felt the finger nails digging into her arms. Her bruised head now featured duct tape and messy hair adorned with twigs and clods of dirt. Drops of blood dried in place on her face. As her brain began to clear, it sent her garbled pain-like messages as she felt the blows to the back of her head. She was coming to. *I 'm being dragged across the forest floor,* she realized. *But where am I exactly?*

The pain in her arms swelled and she feared they would be pulled from their sockets as the two men drug her faster through the endless woods. "Won't work, we are too far behind schedule," Razier said; as they picked their way down the windfall thicket in the dense western Washington forest east of Seattle. "Why did you do that, now we don't have enough help? Razier added.

The other man, the disgusting one with the tattoo, the one pulling on Sherry's left arm said little. He pulled and prodded her body over, under and around the hundreds of downed trees of the large mass of downed trees. Some of the logs were nearly two feet in diameter and rested another foot off the ground. The bark worked like rough sandpaper against Sherry's exposed and irritated skin.

Finally this foul man grunted to Razier, "She can't be over one hundred twenty pounds, she feels like two hundred."

Sherry had heard his voice before. She thought, *I have to remember who he is, I know, I know his voice. I have seen this guy before. I saw that tattoo before, on this guy!* Then all the lights went out for Sherry.

As the two men dragged her over a large downed cedar tree, Kareem lost his grip on her upper arm and she tumbled four feet onto a large rock hitting her head. She lost consciousness.

After nearly an hour, almost exhausted the two men emerged onto a mud and gravel logging road. They had arrived still dragging their unwilling baggage along the side of the gravel road. Without warning, a red Jeep Cherokee emerged from around the corner ahead. It slid to a halt 10 feet away. Razier and the tattooed guy drug Sherry's battered body to the back of the rig and deposited her into the Jeep. She looked like a stained and tattered rag doll snatched from the bottom of a trash pile. Kareem slammed the door shut. As the dust began to roll north on the road, Sherry was dreaming, or was she beginning to put things together? She still wasn't sure. She had a lot of time to think because she was bound and lying in the back of a Jeep bouncing down a forest service road somewhere in the state of Washington.

CHAPTER 2

NOVEMBER 22, 2000, JAIL TIME

Outside the jail the rain continued to fall on the cold wet sidewalks as clerks, parking attendants and various other workers filed past. They paid little attention as they hurried by the concrete and steel buffer that shielded them from the anger, fear and hostility that waited just behind the walls. Inside Carlos Castilano sat cross legged on the pad of the cot in one of the King County cells.

Carlos was a rough and cocky, Spanish and American citizen. He was born in the United States but lived most of his life in Spain. His father was a Spanish diplomat, who had been serving in the United States when Carlos was born. The large J shaped scar on his right cheek betrayed the crazy life Carlos lived. The scar on his face was the souvenir given by a street thug who did not take lightly to Carlos and his unpaid gambling debt.

He was recently jailed after being plucked off the green water of Puget Sound with another man, Hadamid Zucara. Zucara's citizenship was unknown and Zucara was not talking to anyone. The two men had been locked up less than two weeks after they were unleashed from the log raft and lifted from the cold waters.

At the far corner of the cell in which Carlos sat, a spider worked feverously on a small web. A slight smile was evident on Carlos's normally sullen and dower face as the spider added another thread. While he was trapped in a web himself, Carlos thought he was smarter than most of the dimwits in the place. After all he was one of the special people. He had the right to look down on these unfortunate misfits because he was not part of their simple and dreadful existence. His entire life someone had been there to get him out of a jam.

While he had been in a lot of scrapes he was sure that the big guy would get him out shortly. After all, he had a "master's degree" and he was a great programmer. He remembered putting the chip in the tower of the DECmate III computer at Cedarvale High School. He remembered how dumb the clerk at the school was to leave her access code taped to the bottom of her keyboard.

What a nit wit, he thought. She was just a clerk and obviously overpaid at that. She didn't know that she was now part of his plan. All it should take, just a few keystrokes and the specified sequences of zero's and ones would begin to do their magic. He was confident that his success was already assured.

As he looked back at the little spider in the corner, he saw an altogether different creature in his mind's eye. Unlike the one working in the corner of his cell, this spider was underneath the clerk's desk in the school where he had deposited his chip. Like the bug in his mind, his work was done. He planted the chip in a similar way; the mother spider under the desk planted her cocoon home to a thousand eggs. Out of her very own body she expelled the life containing package, at just the right time, in just the right place.

In this case he was at that moment the desk predator. Lost in the vision of his own fantasy, Carlos could see in his twisted mind, the secretary walk to her desk, turn on the computer and suddenly stroke by stroke the infant messages begin spreading out across the copper wires, through the silver connections and ultimately onto the web. This network connects computer to computer, building to building and system to system. She is unwittingly unleashing thousands of bits of information.

Just like the unsuspecting custodian who opened the hidden cocoon as the broom banged awkwardly under the desk; this clerk unknowingly releases thousands of hidden symbols, each containing a specific instruction. Not at all unlike the baby arachnids each on a tiny wire-like stream of protein molecules; the clerk opens the electronic cocoon, stroke by stroke.

Carlos sees the new life forms begin to spread across the office slowly at first, they gain speed and size as they continue to feather out. Each spider moves along with the assistance of personal transport vehicles. Some of the tiny spiders ride on the cuff of an unsuspecting student's pants. Others hang on a small wire, ride to the corner of the room driven by a small breeze. The protein wires serve as lifelines that swing the life forward until thousands of new webs are formed. They develop within the office furniture. He sees them crawling out the door, down the street and across the city.

He was spellbound as he watched the small web master in the cell continue its work. In his fantasy he sees insect armies moving across the vast woodlands. They set up their own little web traps. Each soldier grabs a few ensnared victims. Like the hatch of tiny gnats or flies bursting out to momentary freedom only to be caught in the web. They are entangled and eventually captured by the, already waiting hungry insect.

For these few moments, Carlos was this mature spider that released his life form onto the World Wide Web. He almost smelled the dollars as they were snatched; one dollar here, one dollar there,

$50,000 here, $50,000 there, trickling in from a variety of locations throughout the country hidden in the network.

In his dream, new codes re-task actions so that money is sent from a school to a bank. The money moves from this bank to another. Ultimately the money trickles out of the Federal Treasury and the national network of monetary systems. In the end, the money flows into the specified centrally controlled bank networks. As planned, the money is delivered to the jihadists' cause. It arrives electronically at locations described in the pre-determined programs.

It is my design, I am the master, and he smiled.

Carlos had done his job, he was a good soldier. As he sat on his tiny bed he paid homage to the accomplishment. He was in charge. Now even in his cell he was on top again. Even though he felt imprisoned, he was in power. He laughed out loud. He was celebrating in his mind with his partners, some who would never be suspected.

Dollars are gnats; caught in the various schools and city offices in small gnat sized bites; *the rewards of my bug like ingenuity, a tiny rounding error.*

He didn't know that his little spider's nest had been plucked from its hiding place and that his was now, the life of a grieving parent. He didn't know that his little cocoon had already been raided.

Suddenly he was shaken from his self-indulgent fantasy by the loud cries of other inmates. "Shut up your bum," one guy yelled.

"Put a cork in it," another growled.

Now he was forced to confront the truth, he was not in control, he was not the master, he was the gnat. His brief celebration turned to fear. Fear that he might be forced to face the fact. The reality that he did, in fact, strangle that poor agent in Las Palmas.

What might happen if I am sent back to Spain?

His day in court was fast approaching. Slowly his smile turned into a toothless frown. Slowly his eyes turned away from the spider, gradually his shoulders sagged and pushed his head forward and down. He now looked like the defeated and down trodden; the ones he so despised.

A

Less than mile away, in the dank and dreary downstairs apartment just off First Avenue, the rumble of trains and the sounds of harbor ships did not distract Henry Falowitz from his duties. He was finishing what he thought to be an excellent plan. The shadowy figure from which he had received the first $1,000 was to bring him his final payment in just a few short minutes. He had written in what he felt was fine detail the elements of his dry ice fog machine and dry ice blaster.

He knew that the fog machine would work because he had adapted the plan from the exact same idea that he had used just a few months earlier. He had been asked by his Masters Committee chair, Dr. Wizen, to design the machine for the University of Washington Drama production Phantom. He saw for a moment, how the fog filled the stage, as the phantom rowed across singing "The Music of the Night".

He was less comfortable with the blaster. He knew he should have done more testing. He had already been warned that as a scientist, it is irresponsible to rely on plans based on hopes and hunches. He didn't have the time to do the right thing. He wasn't even sure he was doing things properly. There was no parametric testing sequence. There were really no results at all.

He simply copied the calculations from a book. The blaster, he guessed might create just enough energy to break glass and to blow out bolts buried an inch in concrete if and only if the water in the container was near the boiling point and if there was precisely three hundred cubic centimeters of dry ice in the container. He had run the calculations repeatedly. The calculations were nothing more than hunches. He hoped that the amount he specified was the right volume needed to freeze the water and create the required pressure to send the pellets from the cone well beyond the speed required to blast out the glass and free the bolts. At least that is what his calculations suggested.

He was the hasty designer. He was the hack. He looked up at the water stained ceiling.

It should work, it is possible, he thought.

He was to create, and in return he could earn a quick $5,000; a lot of money for a chemical engineering, grad student of limited means. In addition, the vile of pulverized and dried apple seeds and peach pits were easy to produce for a "chemical wizard" like he. It was the extra bonus. For just a brief second he wondered what the items would be used for. Yet, since he had been asked by Mr. Razier his old high school teacher to "help out a friend," it had to be alright. That's what he thought.

Anyway it is just dry ice and the cyanide is a compound any dummy can get.

Just then he heard a knock outside his dingy apartment door.

"Yes," he said.

"Do you have it," a voice replied.

"Here it is," Falowitz said as he opened the door attempting to get a good look at his employer.

The satchel was grabbed from his hand as Falowitz looked down at the role of $100 bills now rolling across the cracked and uneven vinyl floor of his room. That was that. In that short instant the highly anticipated meeting Falowitz had been looking forward to, was over and he still had not seen his boss's face. He knew no more of the plan or what would be the outcome.

CHAPTER 3

December 9, 2000, Trial Motions

Mixed snow and rain fell on the courthouse roof as another day was beginning. Inside, people were filling the court room off of Fifth and James streets, in the governmental plaza not far from the Seattle I-5 freeway. In attendance not only were the local lookie-lieus, but also a large group of area and national press and other media types. The court provided reminders on firearms and cell phone use in the court room on the board outside. The reader board outside court room 7A also said, "State v Zucara special set, pre-trial motion and State v Castilano special set pre-trial motion." On the same reader board was a court docket.

The attorneys representing the Feds would argue that Carlos Castilano, a US citizen, should be tried in the District of the State of Washington for the lessor crime of trespassing and computer hacking as well as attempted theft of government property. On the other side, the Spanish team of four attorneys was prepared to argue that Castilano should be handed over to Spanish authorities for "Asesinato en Primer Grando." Specifically, they would argue that

14

the murder of a maritime agent on Las Palmas a territory of the Spanish Government was a matter of primary importance. As such all other charges must fall in line behind the requirements of Spanish law. The Spaniards were set to argue that their case should take precedence over all other matters.

The matter of Zucara was not as straight forward. The Zucara case was different in that he had not spoken since he was discovered floating on a raft in Puget Sound. It was not clear as to his national origin. Yet the Spanish representatives planned to argue that he was a material witness in the Castilano case. His testimony was critical and as such was subject to Spanish jurist prudence. Secondly he was to be tried for conspiracy to commit murder.

The sound of repeated gavel strikes gradually dominated all other sounds within the room. For a moment there was silence then the words "all rise, hear ye, hear ye, in the Washington Superior Court the honorable Judge Dustin J. Blice presiding."

The puffy faced judge dressed in black, walked over to his elevated oak desk, put on his horn rimmed glasses, opened a dark blue loose leaf notebook and slowly sank into his oversized leather chair.

"Be seated," was heard, yet the judge did not raise his eyes from the notebook.

"Today because time is of the essence and our Spanish friends came a long way we are going to handle things, a little differently. We are here today to consider whether this court is the appropriate venue for two individuals, Carlos Castilano, and Hadamid Zucara. Any recommendations on how we proceed," the judge said.

A strong and confident yet adolescent looking woman walked to the lectern. "Your honor, the County has reason to believe that both individuals were responsible for trespassing and tampering and attempted theft of school district property. In addition, it is our considered opinion they may also be party to the kidnapping of a school teacher or two. And as such should be held in the county Jail until such time as other proper charges can be prepared," the strawberry blond female attorney stated.

At this time, the tall blue suited federal prosecutor added, "We do not disagree."

"What is your position on this matter?" the judge asked the team representative of the Spanish Counselors.

"Your honor," the tall attorney from Seattle with long flowing silver hair began. "While we well understand and empathize with the King County position, we have filed with this court a demand for both individuals to be remanded to the proper Spanish authorities so that they may be brought to trial in the matter of the brutal killing of a Spanish harbor control agent. Whom they then dragged out to sea and left to rot. We need justice for the friends and family of this great and wonderful man, Mister Garcia. Mr. Garcia was bludgeoned and strangled without mercy while at his post in Las Palmas, Canary Island. He suffered a cruel and ugly death. Then he was set loose to decompose at sea by these evil and disgusting people. When he was found his skin had been eaten off his bones by sea birds. His eyes were plucked out of their sockets. Can you imagine the horror? This matter is of extreme importance and urgency. We have signed statements by eye witnesses and others, as well as camera surveillance data that can implicate both individuals in the matter," He added. "So we are asking the court to dismiss the cases without prejudice. This will allow the Spanish representatives to prosecute the matter and provide proper justice for these individuals. In any case the State and or Federal Governments in the US may refile at a later date," He said.

The judge got up from his desk and stated. "I will consider the matter and give you my ruling by noon tomorrow."

The bailiff was heard to say, "All rise, court will now be in recess, the court will reconvene tomorrow the 10th day of December 2000 at 10:00 AM."

CHAPTER 4

December 9, 2000, Mesa Verde

The sun's rays intensified the heat as they shown through the window of the wagon. It was a source of comfort for Sherry. It warmed and soothed what was now a body full of bruises. She had made too many stops along the way. The keepers were not easy on her. She had been beaten and tossed into a garage. She was awaked with her face lying in a mixture of sand and oil. She was led into a dingy room where she listened to the driver and tattooed guy talk about how they would pull out her nails one at a time. The tattooed guy stepped on her hand twisting his foot as he ground it into the floor. She did not give him the satisfaction of so much as a whimper. However this time she was completely humiliated and demeaned.

At one stop, that very day the driver grabbed her and pressed hard against her. Surprisingly, Razier grabbed him by the neck and shoved him away as he warned, "If there is a next time you won't live to regret it."

Sherry was driven to the edge mentally and she lost track of any notion she might have about her location. She knew she was a very long way from the forest service road east of Seattle, Washington. Life did not change as the rear hatch door of the late model Jeep Cherokee was suddenly thrown open.

Dizzy from the numerous blows to the head, Sherry was also groggy from the lack of food and the inability to sleep. Her body had naturally shut down all but the most important functions. Life was now nothing more than a series of disjointed dreams and unclear images, a natural response to repeated battering and emotional trauma.

She did, however, hear Razier say, "Get out!"

She slowly scooted on her sore and mud soaked side to the back of the Jeep. She pushed against the mat as her bloody and chafed elbow shot pangs of pain to her aching head.

"I need water," she begged.

Chocking and gasping Sherry felt warm water gushing over her mouth. She swallowed and gulped as the warm water stopped flowing.

She heard the guy with the tattoo laugh as he said, "had enough?"

Razier Impatiently grunted, "Get out!"

The black hood was again placed over her face. She had become accustomed to this procedure. She recalled how she had been prepared for mistreatment by her handlers. The hood, she remembered, served many purposes including an aid in disorienting the individual and as a tool of intimidation. Each time she was moved the cover was placed over her face. It was removed from time to time. With the black material over her face she had no idea of her whereabouts. She searched for the ground with her outstretched feet but she couldn't feel it. Suddenly she felt a blow to the back of her head. She was propelled forward uncontrollably. She winced as she felt her jaw and feet hit the hard surface of the ground nearly simultaneously.

"Grab her," Razier snipped.

KNIGHT JUSTICE

Sherry felt the sting of gravel piercing the skin of her legs. At the same moment she heard the sound of spinning tires on gravel.

It must be the Jeep speeding away or changing locations, she thought. Her bruised and sore arms felt the pain as her limbs bounced across undeveloped terrain.

"We have got to get her down the shaft before dark." She heard Razier order.

"I am pulling as fast as I can." Sherry heard.

"Where are you taking me?" She managed to ask.

"Shut it," Razier said as Sherry felt the rocks and small brush scrape her feet.

We are going down a steep grade. She began to feel the ground shake. Then there was a rumble that increased to a roar and then near silence as she heard the snorting and baying of horses. Not one or two, it was more like 50.

"Your ride is waiting for you." The other guy said to Sherry.

He grabbed her like a sack of potatoes and threw her over the back of a domestic pony measuring about 13 hands.

"Great, our work is almost done." Razier said with a smile.

"These mustangs are a welcome sight." The other guy said.

"What a great idea, training a bunch of horses and then cutting them in with the wild mustangs here at Mesa Verde."

Mesa Verde, Sherry thought, *we are in the four corners area.*

"The big man doesn't miss any details does he?" Razier suggested.

"Perfect plan," the other guy said with a smile on his pocked and scared face.

Razier said, "You would come a running too if you knew you were going to get oats and carrots."

"Can you tell which are wild and which are domestic horses?" The tattooed guy said.

"I wonder how he kept the domestics separate from the others?" Razier questioned, nearly to himself.

Sherry was fixated on the man's voice. The sound of his voice rang over and over in her head. She had heard it before. As she struggled to remember where she had heard his voice, she suddenly, began to have some clarity. She recalled that she was back in the morning briefing years before. She saw the dingy chairs and well used oak desk in the NYPD precinct.

"Follow and report back on the movements of these scum bags," the duty officer croaked out. Her mind was on fast forward. She had already seen these guys drop off their cargo, two young girls, to a small dress shop off the corner of Forty Fifth Street. She followed the disgusting druggies to Branigan's bar. She had called for backup but as usual the thrill of the chase placed her in harm's way. She waded into the mess against protocol. She was out there alone as she had been so many times before. She knew that her partner would get there. Besides, she worried that these low lives might have identified her and slipped out the back door undetected.

She just walked in and sat down in the smoke filled, cedar paneled room. As luck would have it, within a few seconds Gahenna broke loose. Time slowed as she saw in vivid detail, bodies randomly propelled across the room; a dark wooden chair traced an arc across the rustic tables then burst into light and dark pieces as it crumpled against an immovable wall. She shook as a guy pounded another man's head to the ground. The force caused his head to squash as if it were a bouncing ball filmed in slow motion. Frightened yet confident, she waited for her opportunity. As the fight came to her, she kicked one gangly guy right on the lateral knee ligament and he folded like a paper doll. She stumbled as she grabbed the money filled canvas bag and started for the side room door.

Unfortunately for her, the instant she started through, the door was being pushed open by her partner and the rest of the agents. She was smacked hard right in the head. What she got out of it was a nose job and a promotion. What the thugs got was hard time. Was this voice, the voice she was now hearing, the voice coming from the tattooed guy, that of an agent or just another random con-man? She was not sure. *Finally it all makes sense. I have seen that tattoo before and I could never forget your raspy voice. You are one of the smugglers I busted years ago.*

Then without hesitation and in loud and rapidly forming words she yelled, "You are Bas Boyd, I busted you."

"You guessed it, ya win, now you get to pay for the time I spent In Leavenworth." Boyd snarled. "You think you're in pain now, wait till we get done with ya, Icy Veins. You ain't much now are ya? Hunched over the back of a horse like a corpse is a good start for you."

It was nearly dark when the pack train made its way to what looked like a small pile of rubble near the top of a mesa at the end of a box canyon. Sherry could barely breathe as she was stretched across the back of a dirty horse. She was somewhere some many hours and a number of days from the beginning of her nightmare.

It smells like pinion pine and junipers and it is very hot.

It was hot at least for December, by Seattle standards.

The small pieces of blouse that she had managed to tear off and drop as she lay on the ground, she hoped someone might find between the tracks of the Jeep. She was now just a few miles from where the Jeep stopped.

"Think it is dark enough?" Boyd asked.

"I think so," Razier said.

Sherry heard the sound of small boulders scratching across the ground. She counted three men moving the stones. With as little movement as possible she slowly tore off another piece of her blouse and held it in her hand. Then she slid feet first towards the ground. She landed with a thud. Her elbow hit the ground at the same time as her hip. She did not feel pain as the dehydration continued to numb her brain.

"Let's go tough gal," Bas Boyd grunted.

Sherry was motionless unable to get up. A boot to the ribs was the next blow. Sherry felt the pain this time, and instinctively moved her duct taped hand to protect her rib. Then she noticed what she was sure was blood coming from her side. She took the small cloth she had in her hand and rubbed it against her skin. She moved her hands to the side of what she now recognized as a path. Slowly she slid the cloth under a fist sized rock. She hoped a person might stumble upon it and know that there was someone needing help.

Just then she felt hands grabbing her upper arms and again her feet were banging on sharp rocks. The cool air coming out of the cave slightly revived her as Razier and Boyd dragged her down into the cave's entrance shaft. It was nothing more than a crude opening in a sharp out cropping of rocks. Her captors cleared the few rocks that disguised the opening of the cave moments earlier. As such the musty smell of mold and mildew combined with the smell of juniper and pine wafted by Sherry's nostrils.

Sherry noticed that the jarring stopped as her feet began to slide more easily over the cool smooth stones. In her confused and pained state she forced herself to note the distance she traveled. *Nearly thirty feet down a pretty steep slope.* Sherry's body was released with a thud.

"Let's get out of here," she heard Razier say.

The next sounds she heard were receding footsteps moving slowly more distant. She heard the scratch of a horse hoof on stone. Sherry also thought she heard the sounds of stones grinding against each other. She could not make sense of what they were doing and saying, as she fought to maintain rational thought. After what she guessed was no more than 40 minutes, the sounds of scratching and grinding, horses and men, grunting and swearing, were over. She slept.

CHAPTER 5

December 10, 2000, Give Take

The rain drops glistened as they landed on the window ledge just outside the small musty office window in the office. Judge Blice had been in his chambers all morning. He had read and reread the briefs submitted by the Spanish and United States Feds. Both parties provided ample argument and solid legal framework. He was not convinced as to which way to rule.

Zucara is the easy one. All he is possibly guilty of is trespassing and tampering with State property. Besides who knows where this kid is from, or what other craziness he has been into. He could turn into a real nightmare with no end. I don't need that. I can send him back without a big outcry. He thought.

Now Castilano is a mule of different pedigree. If I let him go, I will be in for a huge political problem. I can hear the protestors now. They would turn me into a Casper within minutes. At my age I don't need this. Besides If I let Zucara go I allow the Spaniards to try him for conspiracy or whatever the heck they want. At least he is out of our hair. We can keep Castilano and get him his justice. Besides he is a US citizen. Once we try him they can have him if they want. Yeah, that's the best for everyone and that is what I'll do.

He jotted down a few notes, grabbed the briefs and headed for the door. As he walked into the court room he was struck by just how significant the case was becoming. Not only was it attracting national attention but the Spaniards by their legitimate interest, added an international flavor to the evermore bizarre setting.

As he walked in, he heard the words: "All rise."

Sitting down and out of habit said, "You may be seated." He wasted no time.

"Mr. Zucara please stand." He said, "You have been charged with trespass and tampering with state property. While I am persuaded that there is enough evidence to try you for the charges against you, I believe that you must first answer to the Spaniards. I therefore dismiss the pending charges with prejudice and remand you over to the Spanish authorities.

"Are there any questions?" The judge waited a solid 30 seconds.

"Hearing none I so direct and let the record show." He slammed his gavel down.

Looking like a deer in the headlights, Zucara was ushered out of the court by the Spanish authorities.

The judge said, "Mr. Castilano please stand."

Carlos Castilano stood with a smirk on his face. The large, wide, scar on his cheek was clearly evident in the bright courtroom light.

"I have determined that the Spanish have not provided enough legal precedent to override the protections and interests that are provided you as a US citizen. Therefore, It is my order that you will be held by the American authorities for trial to face the charges against you. The matter of bail is to be determined at a later date. Are there any questions?" He paused. "It is so ordered."

"You may appeal if you want," he said. He pounded his gavel. Immediately the courtroom burst into a cacophony of sound and action. Reporters hustled out of the court. Carlos stood and stared at the judge as the judge walked through the antechamber door and disappeared.

CHAPTER 6

DECEMBER 11, 2000, RESERVATIONS REGRETS

The low angle of the eastern sunrise hindered the life giving rays as they began to excite the surface of the ground not far from Sherry. However, she was unable to benefit from the warmth. After an unceremonious horseback ride across a steep mesa Sherry was entombed by Razier, Boyd and others. She had been given just enough water to survive a few days. Frankly these men could not care less whether she survived. Without an extraordinary will she would already be gone.

The warmth of the sun did not penetrate the cool cave in which she was abandoned. Yet the cave was, in fact, helpful to her. The stone floor served to awaken her. She was gradually becoming aware of the sound of drops of water trickling in the darkness behind her. She wondered how long she had been lying there. For all she knew she could of been there a day, a week, or a month. She just wasn't sure.

"Thank God I will live." She mumbled slowly.

Blood was coursing through her head as she recalled the ordeal she had been through. The pain in her knees was almost impossible to bear.

"Is this life I chose, all there is?" She asked.

No one responded. She did not need to be reminded that she was alone in the dark. The musty, cool air helped to reinforce for her that she was in a cave. She could feel the tape cutting into her wrists. She also felt that her ankles were bound somehow.

"You can't do this!" She yelled.

No response.

"I know you're here." She announced.

No response.

She continued, just as a child might continue, to kick and punch a candy machine that had taken the last dollar and given nothing in return.

"You'll pay for this." She asserted.

No response.

"What makes you think you can treat me like this?" She asked.

No response.

"How long are you keeping me here?" She asked.

No response.

After repeated demands, exhausted and trapped she fell asleep. In a dream she was walking into her childhood home. It was just east of National Street in North Springfield, Missouri. If you even could call it a home. It was a trailer. Just a few blocks that separated her trailer from the beautiful campus of Evangel College. She had wandered over to the campus on a few occasions. There she would sit down under a big oak tree and watch the students bustle from the chapel to class. She heard them argue over the best approach to calculate power using the Nernst equation. She did not know what a kilocalorie was.

Someday I will, she thought as she watched some guys toss a Frisbee back and forth. She saw herself as one of these fortunate people. She reflected on the mostly attractive and careless kids that made up the college campus population.

She skipped home all excited and happy. She danced into the trailer park and noticed how few oak trees there really were. Just one or two trees separated the small metal boxes from one another. She was living in one of these metal boxes. Now she was in her room. This box was her jail. The room she shared with her sister was about eight feet square. She shared her single twin bed with her little sister. There was just enough space between the end of the bed and the wall to get to the window. The window was her favorite place to dream. From the window she could see the small private airfield. The landing strip was where she watched small planes emerge from the sky, like birds soaring in the wind. She could see them as if they were just outside her window. What freedom they had! Watching these winged machines come and go from heaven's gates renewed her hope for a better life. A life she lived in her mind. In these fleeting snippets of time were images of her childhood; in reality it was not at all that fun or wonderful.

She saw and heard the ugly reality of it all. She fought off the urge to cover her ears as she heard her father yelling. The vulgar language did not bother her, she was used to it. Besides, he was not agitated at her. He was targeting her mother.

Sherry was spared most of the time, because she was the good kid, "daddy's little chocolate headed cookie."

She smelled the stench of alcohol on his breath; she saw the fear in her mother's eyes. That is what she saw in her mind. She had had it!

The last thing she heard was her mom scream, "I can't take it," then the back of his hand across her mother's cheek.

The smack sounded like a branch breaking in a windstorm. She saw the tears.

She heard him say the words, "I'm sorry!" Her dad slowly relaxed his fist.

It was the never ending nightmare. Sherry could still feel the vibrations of the door behind her. Her legs propelled her forward. This time she was really gone. She remembered running, just running.

Sherry remembered how she had somehow ended up on the gray limestone steps of the chapel on the Evangel College campus. She was still crying when she ran right into the arms of a nursing student who took her, a frightened little ten-year old to St. John's Hospital: St. John's, of the same order that founded a network of Hospitals. Through her life, Sherry had been admitted to some of them. She tried to remember the names, yes, Sisters of Mercy. An image of the face of the founder, a strong Irish woman, floated by seemingly in the clouds. It was the face of Catherine McAuley. She was one of Sherry's hero's. McAuley was the founder of Sisters of Mercy. The organization was dedicated to serve the needs of poor women and children. Catherine McAuley, lived with Quakers. She became a Catholic Sister in order to continue her commitment to the down trodden.

In Sherry's case, a movement started in Ireland had literally saved her life in the United States of America. Sherry replayed the sights and sounds of her long bus ride to the State of Washington. That is where she met Jake. He had not heard the details until recently and frankly still had trouble believing much of the story anyway. Through the Advocacy of the Sisters of Mercy and those at Evangel College she was rescued from her steel box in Springfield. Her brain cried out for a resolution of the breach. As usual there was no resolution. It was her extraordinary inner strength and strong belief that propelled her forward through a difficult and troubling life. This cave prison was just another bump in the road. Granted it was a large one even for her.

⋏

Sherry shared her dream with Jake. As her dream churned on, she saw people, Catholics and Protestants. She saw lots of people, Muslims, Jews, Mormons, Lutherans, Hindus and Buddhists. She saw a lion and a lamb; what did it all mean? She was on a bus with all these people. They were throwing bread to shabbily dressed people along the road.

She looked up to see the huge bus was driven by all these people. The people she knew and trusted took turns at the wheel. The drivers were the ones who cared for and taught her. They came from all walks of life. They not only drove the bus they threw the bread. Christian was there. She saw me in a white polo shirt and red and white tennis shoes. They all begged her to take the wheel of the now driverless bus. She just couldn't manage the wheel. It was too cold, it was too big. She was so cold she just could not help. People were screaming. She was in the dark. She was sitting on a seat of stone. It felt like cold hard ground.

She was prostrate on the stone bus seat. She wanted to wake up but she was tired. It was cold and the bus was out of control. It was going off the cliff. Then she was again awake. She was not in Missouri. She was not in Seattle. She was not on a bus. She was in a cave. It was obvious that she was lying on a smooth stone floor. Some kind of stone, a stone like limestone.

⋏

Troubled by what she had just experienced in her dream, she inched backward like a snake for approximately ten feet. What was she to make of the dream? Was she losing a grip? She found a cold damp wall. Gradually, she made her way up the side of the wall, her fingers leading the way. She rocked back and forth in an effort to right herself. Now her back was against the wall. It felt moist and cold.

Then she screamed, "help!"

Again and again she screamed to no avail. She only heard the echoes as the cry's bounced off the stone walls. The only sound she heard was that of water dripping a few feet from her. Using palms on the ground, as a crutch and by flexing and relaxing her buttocks muscles, Sherry slowly inched her way towards the sound of dripping water. Her right hand still taped to her left she immediately felt standing water.

She instinctively leaned over and began to sip the cool liquid. She didn't even stop and worry about giardia or the many possible contaminants she might be introducing into her body. The drive for survival was guiding her now. She continued to suck up the water until she felt pressure in her abdomen. It tasted so good. She just laid there for a moment. Almost immediately, she began to gain strength. She was now more aware of the tape on her wrist. It cut into her skin and it hurt.

She could taste blood as she bit into the now familiar feeling duct tape lashed to her wrists. Gnawing and tearing with her teeth she gradually freed her hands. She sighed as she felt the freedom of her hands. Hands that had been lashed together for what she knew was more than a week. Next she slowly pulled the tape from her eyes, flinching as each layer of tape removed hair from her head. Once the tape was off her eyes she was still unable to see.

Am I blind or is there no light? She could not tell. As she sat listening to the water drip she thought she might be detecting movement of the surface of the water. It was as if she was getting a vibration from the water itself.

KNIGHT JUSTICE

Sherry began to work the tape around her ankles. Her fingers burned as she struggled to unfasten the tape. Ever so slowly she unraveled layer by layer. She barely noticed the pounding of her head, as her desire to be free of the tape was paramount. She slowly freed her ankles. Once liberated she felt the urge to call out again, "help!" she screamed at the top of her lungs. Expecting no answer she prepared to yell again. At that very moment, time stood still. She felt the impulses of the shiver that ran from the back of her neck to her toes.

"What the!" she yelled.

CHAPTER 7

January 6, 2001, School Daze

The snow shimmered in the sunlight as the cold white blanket covered the ground. For me it provided no warmth. While I learned a great deal the past few weeks; I was beginning to grow weary of the constant routine. Up at 5:30 AM, stager into the kitchen, eat my frosted flakes and then head to the gym for hours of fitness and self-defense training. Then off to a series of history and in my case, psychoanalysis seminars. I was fortunate to have been trained by the best and brightest in the world. It really seemed like a steady stream of who's who in the world of psychological warfare and personal assessment.

Today we were in Alexandria, Virginia in a make shift meeting room in the basement of the Florencia restaurant just off 17th St. N.W. Five other "students" and myself were in our final seminar on knightly ethics; not the most engaging of topics. Flags placed at strategic locations behind the podium, hung from brass poles. The banners promoted phrases including:

Knowing rightly
Responding timely
Investing justly

KNIGHT JUSTICE

These reminded me almost constantly of my obligations. Christian D. Poincy esquire, the Major Sigma Knight was opening his last lecture on the ethics of the modern agents. I had been sitting there so long that the blood had drained from my rear. I arrived early and had time to do a little decompressing. I was sitting there thinking about my recent besting of all the FBI and CIA recruits the afternoon before in the obstacle course.

I recalled the details in fond mental snippets. I climbed the rope with the 100 pound dummy held by my legs. My arms burned as I pulled ahead of the guy next to me. He was a twenty-five year-old former Navy Seal who thought he was pretty tough. I skirted the 15 foot wall, slid almost freefall as the rope sizzled in my hands. I hit the ground with a thud and ran the 100 yards to the finish with the dummy bouncing on my back. In my focused mind, the dummy was really Sherry. For now, first place wasn't bad for a thirty-two year-old. In this group of new recruits, I was one of the old guys. All were destined to become agents but I was the only St. Johns of Malta novice.

When the former seal walked up and said, "Your all-right Jake," I felt I had arrived.

Most of the others saw him as the top dog. He was the one that gave me a lot of hype about my dark eyes, "the eyes of a spy, with the hair of a Scot, and the dress of a beach bum; what a combo," he said, when I first met him. I had no real interest in what he or anyone else thought. I was here for one purpose. That purpose was to be as prepared as I could be when we rescued Sherry.

It was hard to believe I was sitting in one of my final training seminars listening to Christian. *Enough of the nostalgia, I need to focus on the lecture.* Finally my mind was tuned to Christian and his words.

He said, "It is not enough to have right on your side, you must also be in tune with who will be, who is and who has been. We listen with our soul as well as our five senses and that, my friends, is different for each of us."

What he discussed made me think of Sherry. She is the only other person who listens with her soul. I had to admit she was becoming an obsession for me. She was the reason I was so driven. I heard Christian say something. Frankly I can't remember what he said but I could not contain myself any longer.

I was stuck on Sherry. "Was it God's will for Sherry to be taken by these extortionists," I blurted out.

Christian began. "Take a deep breath Jake, there are things we just don't understand; that's the way it is. As you have learned the past few months we all must prepare. We must be ready to be advocates, and yet we must be disciplined. It is of little or no positive effect to strike out unprepared against those whom we are aggrieved."

The others in the room seemed less interested than I was. While they were aware of some of the details of the entire situation in Seattle, many of them were frying their own fish. Christian chose that moment to dismiss the group. "You guys have had enough today." He said with a smile.

He had a great way sensing what was happening around him and taking the right corrective action. However, for me things were moving too slow. I had been trained to get things done. You know the boot strap kind of approach. I always liked to get it going then, take whatever comes as it comes. So for me there was far too little action.

Just as the room cleared I said to Christian, "It is easy to say we need to be sensitive to the right timing. The way I see it, we are wasting valuable time talking when we should be taking action. I for one feel that I am ready to do what I can to find her." I said in a loud and assertive voice that even surprised me.

Christian, not missing a beat calmly replied, "And what exactly would you do at this point."

Stunned by his cool response, I paused. Then in what I thought were carefully chosen words I said, "We need a small force to track down these cowards and bring them to justice."

"Who pray tell are these people and where are they hiding Jake? Do you know?" Christian asked slowly.

I could feel my face heating up and I knew that the color of embarrassment betrayed me. I had been working on the control of my emotions. Just one of the factors associated with the discipline of a knight. That red face, a natural response to anxiety, was something about which Christian had repeatedly reminded me.

"If you expect to be an effective agent you must control your response to your anxieties."

Well easier said than done. "Well sir, I don't know; but you *must* know by now," I finally choked out.

"Jake we have been informed by our friends in Spain that an inmate close to Carlos Castilano says that Sherry is being held in Colorado somewhere. That has not been confirmed as of yet." Christian said.

"When will you know, and more importantly when will I know, exactly so we can mount a rescue?" I queried.

The very real possibility that we might not get Sherry back had been churning within me for weeks. Despite what I was learning from Christian and others I had to ask; more to ease my self-imposed pressure than to get an answer. Christian, a distinguished looking man with silver hair and almost too thin a body looked at me with his penetrating grey blue eyes and walked slowly towards me. He leaned in close so that I could feel his breath on my ear.

"I know how much Sherry means to you and I hope you know that she means as much to me. For now we will have to wait and learn." He whispered. "Trust me, when we know enough and when we are ready we will act."

"What's your guess, will we get her back safely?" I asked.

Christian outlined Sherry's current status. "I think there is a good chance she is safe since we understand that there is a ransom request. In these situations these people want to negotiate in good faith. I know that sounds weird but that's my sense. My point is; you have to learn to work with God's timeline as well as your own. If you don't, you will cause yourself and others more harm than good. By the way Jake, did I tell you that they retrieved the chip from the computer at your school. It looks like it was manufactured in China, stolen and ended up in Iran after a brief stop in North Korea. It has the capacity to extract money from the federal school network."

"How could it?" I asked.

Christian provided what he knew. "Quite simple, he said, it does two things; first it has a code that allows for the data processer to emulate the main frame in Washington, DC. When the school requests a download from the district computer it also contains a Trojan Horse. Because the local schools have access to the main pipes at the local district level they also have access to the state level computers through the same pipes. Once a pipe is open the codes in the Trojan search the financial data bases for access codes.

Now there are fire-walls built in, but the Trojan has the capability to bypass the firewall. As you are well aware, each state in the union has access to the national educational computers in DC. When the Department of Education sends out money to the states to the tune of billions of dollars, it does not check the rounding rules for each state. That is where the second component comes in. When the computer at your school accesses the state system it now accesses the entire pipe to DC. All the chip does is simply adjust the rounding rules. Instead of rounding down it rounds up; once rounded the program adds a dollar. It also provides instructions to send the extra dollar, not to the local bank but to a specific branch. Because so many schools use American's Bank, the bank routing number change would only be detectable to the most astute. This skimmed amount was to wind up in a branch in Southern California.

Fortunately now the feds have the chip and are designing a firewall fix as we speak. Can you imagine what a disaster this might have been? One of the smallest estimates I heard is in the millions. It could be more, possibly even the billions of dollars. Sherry was important to them because she has the background to write codes that allow for transfers from American's Bank to banks in Munich. Now with the chip in the hands of the State Department she is of less value to the terrorists. I have to get her to Munich so she can design a specific fix in case other cells were successful and the damage had been done in other localities. Small state agencies like municipal governments, like cities are also vulnerable. They are connected in much the same manner as I described."

"So that is what the whole thing was really about."

"Correct, and that is all I currently know."

"Can I quote you on that?"

"I didn't say it and you heard it!"

Moments later, as we were leaving, he pulled me aside. "I was told by your physical training instructor that you have learned a lot. Is it true that you are 190 pounds? You are getting pretty buff. Your arms look like the muscles have been covered over with Saran Wrap." Christian said.

"Well ya know I was a college wrestler. I learned martial arts because I wanted to be a better wrestler." I replied.

"Jake were you ever a Cub Scout?"

"You must know that I was an Eagle Scout."

"There comes a point when there are no more arrowheads Jake." He smiled.

I tried not to smile but I knew I needed to slow down a little.

"When are you going to get rid of those old red and white Converse tennis shoes?" He inquired jokingly.

"Does that mean we are ready to mount a rescue attempt for Sherry?" I asked, as we walked up the stairs together.

"One piece at a time, my friend, one piece at a time." He said as he walked towards the main door.

It was the last major session in DC. Christian already informed me that I would soon be off to the final training site. I had no real idea where that site might be. I was told that shortly I would board a plane and be dropped off somewhere to fend for myself. If I passed this final field test then I was ready. I would then be a knight, one of the elite.

"Do you mind if I walk with you to your car?"

"Come along what's on your mind?"

"I just want you to know how much I appreciate your guidance."

"All right, but what else is on your mind?"

"Well to be frank I, I've been preparing for my testimony on the Carlos Castilano trial and I am troubled to say the least. There is something about the Ieke Rollands character that just does not pass the sniff test. I think Rollands knows Castilano." I said.

"Well sure he knows Carlos, who do you think helped us plan and design stratagies to catch Carlos and these guys right in the act? Rollands has been an agent for a long time. You don't get to his level without a lot of tests and checks." Christian said.

"I know that but you must have known a lot of double agents in your day. I have read about how the CIA has been duped time and time again." I said.

"Yes but that's the CIA, we are more careful. I would like to hear more." Christian prodded.

I provided my support in this way. "I have this recurring dream, Rollands is carrying a medieval dagger. You know one of those elk horn handled jobs. He is sitting there sharpening it on a stone. He has this evil smile. Even when he is there to help, I see in his eyes the hint of, well, uh evil. The thing is I never have been able to trust the guy. I know he was there to help us when Sherry disappeared but he never really made sense to me. It was more like he was trying to mess things up. Plus, when I look into those clear blue eyes they twitch just a little and in my work with kids that means watch out there is an unreliable character underneath that dashing facade. I know he is a knight and all."

Christian said, "In the tiny ravines of your mind the truth lays waiting to be discovered. Don't ignore your dreams for in them, you will find the truth, if and only if you sift through the soil long enough to see the grains that are there. Do you follow what I am saying Jake? But as for Rollands he is fine."

He walked on without the slightest glance. I could not quite figure out what he was saying. Even as I struggled with the thought that Ieke was "fine" like powdered grains of sand. I was becoming more confident. As I watched Christian get into his black Escalade, I was feeling better about Sherry and about our chances getting her back. He had a way of instilling confidence in me like none other. Sherry had not been seen or heard of in some time, yet at that moment I really felt she was all right.

CHAPTER 8

JANUARY 8, 2001, NO WITNESSES

D ark storm clouds moved in across Puget Sound. They were driven by a strong westerly wind. The rain had not yet begun to fall. It was Monday morning, the day before Carlos Castilano's trial was to begin. Mr. Weiss's executive secretary was the first to notice the message. It was a slow day. She had been making her last bid on a necklace she hoped to purchase on e-bay.

As she watched the auction clock on her computer screen click to one minute the following message appeared on her screen:

"Trade Sherry Paul for Carlos Castilano"

For an instant, she thought it was some kind of joke. After she attempted to reboot the computer she discovered it was no joke. She immediately summoned her boss Willie Weiss.

In office after office in the area the same exact thing was happening. Simultaneously on computers throughout the city of Seattle and many school districts in the region was the same message. The message showed up on nearly 1000 computers in the Seattle area. It did not appear on all computer screens in the region. The only screens on which the message appeared were those that were logged onto the internet and those that used "internet-navigator" as the internet provider.

The message "Trade Sherry Paul for Carlos Castilano" was written in large letters and the screens were locked. This, as might be imagined, caused a general state of panic and fear throughout the city. A number of ad hoc task forces where thrown together in hopes of finding clues that might lead to the perpetrators. The frozen screens that were not unplugged continued to be locked. There was no immediate solution. What made this situation different from that of Cedervale was that no chips were found in the towers and there were no suspects. In tech support centers around the city phones rang and spontaneous problem solving began.

"We need a no internet use policy," Stanley from business said.

"Are there more Carlos Castiano's out there?" Mary from legal asked.

"Did Carlos get to our system?" Hannah from Personnel added.

"Is our money safe?" Benny from finance questioned.

However it is doubtful that Carlos could have been involved, because he was in the slammer. Unaware, Judge Blice was in his chambers reading updated briefs related to the pending Castilano case. He was abruptly interrupted by the King County Executive Willie Weiss.

"Judge we have a situation here," the executive said.

"Situation?" the judge responded, "what kind of situation?"

"I have been told by my secretary that computer screens throughout the city have shown a message.

The message merely says: "Trade Sherry Paul for Carlos Castilano." The executive said.

"They want to deal!" Blice yelled, "I am in a trial. You know I can't help you with this. What do they think that I am, some sort of hack politician?"

"And who are these people anyway?" Blice added.

"We're not sure," the executive said.

"What do you mean you're not sure?" Blice snapped.

"The message just says it's a trade offer. If you want to respond, we are all right with that. I have spoken with the Mayor and the majority of council and we can make it work." Weiss added.

"Let's just ignore it," Blice suggested.

"It's more complicated than that," the executive stated.

"What do you mean more complicated than that?" The judge asked.

"Well for one thing the screens are all locked up," the executive said. "In addition to that, there are small clocks on this message." The executive explained.

"The clocks are counting down from three hours. We now only have two hours." Weiss warned.

"Then what happens?" Blice asked.

"We don't know."

"Let's get the FBI involved." The judge said.

"Okay will do."

Within minutes news organizations were running to government buildings throughout the city. Within 20 minutes the office of the executive of King County was teeming with agents from the FBI. Behind closed doors the executive was meeting with the FBI's district director.

"Well John, we think we do," the executive said.

"Let's have your secretary type on her computer screen 'no deal'," the director said "I have already begun a tie-in with the federal computers," he continued.

"Okay we are on it." Weiss replied.

They headed out of the room together. As they walked out to the main secretarial pool, the executive walked up to Katy at the large desk behind the others.

"I want you to type in on your screen 'no deal'. Okay?" Weiss directed.

"My screen is locked," Katy replied.

"Try anyway," the executive responded.

"You got it!" Katy said.

She typed in "no deal". Immediately upon her typing those words was the response.

"Now Sherry Paul will cost you $10 million dollars, plus release of Carlos Castiano."

The same message appeared on all computers still plugged in around the city.

"What do I do now?" Katy questioned her boss.

"Type 'no deal' again," the executive said.

She did as instructed.

"Sherry will pay," was the response.

Again the message appeared around the city. After a few minutes, the screens went blank and the system began to operate as if nothing had happened. The executive turned to John, the FBI director "Did you get a trace?"

John replied, "Yes, it came from a computer at the Seattle Public Library, agents are following up with witnesses as we speak."

"We'll get on this right away and see what we can do find out who it came from," the director of the FBI said.

Meantime city business continued as usual. The executive went back to his office and picked up the phone. He dialed Dustin Blice's office.

"Dustin here," was the reply on the others in the line.

"I guess there is no real danger in going ahead with the trial," the executive said.

"Don't worry." Weiss said to Blice.

Blice shot back "If I was the type to worry I would have left here years ago."

Little else happened out of the ordinary that day other than the local media and press had a field day. The trial began Wednesday morning as scheduled. Blice got the trial started with his normal routine which included rushing in at the last moment, sitting at his large desk and piering over his large glasses.

He asked "Madam Prosecutor, will you be calling any witnesses?"

"For the record your honor," The prosecutor of the case against Carlos Castiano said, "We will be calling the following witnesses, Ieke Rollands, Superintendent Seattle Public Schools, Cheryl Apostle, Secretary Cedarvale high school and…" A long list of others included people like traffic director at Atlas Security the company that protected Ceadervale High, as well as teachers and other staff of the high school."

At the time of trial there were no witnessed on the defense list.

CHAPTER 9

January 9, 2001, The Trial

Rain was pelting the streets as the cars carrying workers were jamming the already crowded streets. Inside the jail Carlos was awakened early on the morning of January 9, 2001. His court appointed attorney was standing outside his cell at 6:00 AM. The officer that unlocked the cell scowled at Carlos and the attorney, Mr. Cage walked out with the police escort. Cage was a portly man not even five and a half feet tall. He sprouted thinning dark brown hair with flecks of grey. He sported a full splotchy beard. He was not physically impressive. The group preceded to the metal exit doors and waited for the familiar buzz of the electronic release. After about a two second pause, the door sprung open with a clang. The trio walked out of the jail. Carlos was wearing typical orange prison garb. The other two were wearing wool sport coats.

Carlos, said to his defense attorney, "Let's get some real food."

Mr. Cage turned to the officer and said, "I want to stop for breakfast, I think there is a place right next door. You won't mind Seabucks will you?"

The detective Sgt. turned and nodded his head in agreement. Moments later the three entered Seabucks.

Pulling pants and a shirt from the plain brown bag, Cage suggested, "You might like to change your clothes."

To that, the Officer walked Carlos to the restroom. Once inside the officer attached one handcuff to the bottom rail of the stall rail and the other to Carlos's leg. This allowed Carlos to change his shirt. The officer then underwent the repeat process; only this time it was an arm attached to the toilet. Carlos changed his pants as he loudly protested the mistreatment. He was looking for an audience but the officer seemed unimpressed. Carlos, now reattached to the officer emerged with his orange jumpsuit in hand. Carlos sat down to a scone and a cup of coffee.

Mr. Cage asked, "Might I be alone with Mr. Castilano a few moments?"

The officer stepped away from the table after attaching one cuff to the leg of the table.

Mr. Cage said, "Carlos you must remain silent and positive at all times during the hearing."

Carlos in his cocky way said, "I know what I'm doing here I'm cool."

Mr. Cage said, "It's very important that we put on a good face this morning."

"Okay let's get to it, let go." Carlos said.

Cage nodded to the officer, the officer returned a slight nod then the three headed out to the courthouse just down the street. The white stone pillars and marble floor seemed to squeak with each step. As the doors of the courthouse slammed shut, Carlo's face showed fear for the first time.

The three walked the few steps into the courthouse hall. They made their way through the security scanners and onto the marble of a much wider hall. The sound of their shoes continued to echo as they walked over to the elevator. The three stepped in and the doors

KNIGHT JUSTICE

closed behind. The elevator stopped on the fifth floor and the three got out. After a right turn in a few quick steps they entered the courtroom of Judge Dustin J. Blice.

The jurors as well as many members of the press where already in the court room. The prosecutors were sitting at a narrow desk flipping through paperwork. Mr. Cage and Carlos Castilano took their seats at the left-hand desk.

The bailiff got out of his chair and said, "All rise, the Honorable Dustin J. Blice," as the judge entered the room.

Judge Blice took his position in the large leather chair. He opened a file on his desk and read from a prepared script. "Mr. Castilano you have been charged with trespassing, attempted theft of government property and reckless endangerment."

Mr. Cage then replied, "We are ready for trial your honor."

"Has there been a plea agreement or are we proceeding to trial?" The Judge said.

The Prosecutor said, "At this time, there has not."

He turned to the defense, "Do you have any questions Mr. Cage?"

"No sir we do not."

"How do you plead?" Blice asked.

"Not guilty on all counts your honor," Cage responded.

The judge then said, "Okay anything further?"

There was no response.

The judge replied, "Let the record reflect."

The judge then turned to the prosecutors and said, "Madam Prosecutor is the prosecution ready for the case?"

The County prosecutor, dressed in a black dress, replied, "The County is your honor."

The judge said, "This court will be in recess and will reconvene here at 9 AM sharp in two days for motions in limine. The Judge got up and left the courtroom.

47

Carlos turned to Mr. Cage and said, "What just happened here and where did the judge go?

Cage said, "That is just the way it goes, the fireworks start in two days."

Carlos shot a look of distain, almost a look of pity at Cage. Carlos for the first time thought he might have made a mistake disavowing his family and the considerable resources at his disposal.

CHAPTER 10

JANUARY 10, 2001, VISION QUEST

The sun was beginning to shine through broken clouds. Steam was slightly evident above the puddles on the side walk. I was able to take a moment and look outside because I was ready and a few minutes ahead of schedule. I had been up early and raring to go much before my appointed pickup time. I shipped all my belongings, less the bare essentials, home the day before. The black Lincoln was already waiting as I walked out the door and down the steps of the old manner house turned apartment building. On my back was a small backpack.

The driver an all business type, said, "get in we've got to beat the traffic."

The trip to the airport was uneventful, as was the check-in process. I boarded a flight from Reagan National Airport to Denver Colorado. The approximately three-hour flight was not enjoyable. I was seated in coach. The guy next to me felt the need to foul the air every five minutes or so. I mean this guy smelled like a rotten cheese factory. In addition, he wanted to explain to me all he knew about the air conditioning business. All I could do was think of how much we could use a bit of air conditioning or at least ventilation ourselves. I got up a few times and hung out by the lavatory just to make sure that other passengers must have known who the gasser was. thankgoodness, the flight was just three hours long.

I was impressed by the landing. Denver is known for hard landings, being a mile high. I guess the thin air makes for rougher touchdowns. I was prepared for one and I was ready to cover my nose as I was sure a hard landing might cause a gas leak of intolerable proportions. Instead the pilot greased it on. Upon arrival at the security check point, I was greeted by a tall man with dark hair. The man, wearing black owl eyed glasses, held a sign that stated JR.

I walked up to the man and asked if he had ever traveled the river Jordan.

The man answered, "I have not been there but I've seen pictures."

I then said, "I haven't been there either but I would like to go someday."

This was the preassigned conversation I had been instructed to use.

"Sounds like a great trip," the large man said. He then led me to the waiting black Cadillac Escalade.

We got in the rear seat and the car took off. "Where we headed now?" I asked with a smile.

"You should not be concerning yourself with this kind of thing now," the big guy said. "In time you'll know all you need to know. Just sit back and relax, we have a long ride ahead of us." The driver said.

The sun filtered in through the window as it warmed the leather on the seat. I drifted off to sleep. A few hours later, I awoke as the car pulled off into the parking lot of what I could see was a trailhead. It looked to me like a national forest trail. There were no other cars in the dusty vacant area. I had no idea about the specific location other than that it was south of Denver and a long way south, like hours. The large man seated next to me pushed me out of the car. I landed on the ground with a thud. A day pack was thrown from the vehicle hitting me in the chest.

The car raced off in a cloud of dust. As it left my sight, I noticed that the cloud of tan dust billowing out from behind the dirt caked Cadillac seemed to consume the car. I was alone on a trailhead somewhere in southern Colorado or northern New Mexico, I really was not sure. I sat on the ground for at least five minutes. I wondered if I had made a mistake.

My kids are thousands of miles away. My parents are now expected to raise my two children whom I miss greatly. I quit what I now realize was a pretty great job. And I am in the middle of nowhere, alone with a backpack lying on my chest. I'm here to rescue Sherry, but what do I really know of her. She waltzed back into my life after a decade without contact. She gets me to join this group of Knights that I don't even really know if they exist. I never really have been all alone in woods by myself. Maybe I should just get up walk out to the nearest road. Get back to Denver or Albuquerque, wherever the heck is closest city and get on with my normal life. I could just walk right out this road they drove on and eventually find somebody. It is strange that I haven't seen any sign of life in this area.

Then my thoughts took a sharp reversal. "Well maybe this back country experience could be fun. Besides, this challenge gets me one step closer to saving Sherry." I said in a whisper.

Still not quite sure I was making the right decision; I slowly unzipped the zipper on the top of the pack. I pulled out a plastic thermos filled with water. The little plastic container at the bottom of the pack contained what appeared to be jerky of some sort. I also noticed a small flashlight that had a crank for charging. There was a knife, with about a six inch blade. I also found a multi-tool with cutting edges, pliers and other tools. Wrapped in a small plastic case was a map and compass. I gummed a piece of jerky. As I felt the sting of salt on my tongue, I noticed the map had a big X marked in red with printing that said "you are here."

As I looked closely at the map I saw a number of symbols and various marks. In the center of the map I studied a large red circle. Printed on the map were the following words, "This is your objective."

"Now is the time to figure out what you're made of, Jake!" I said.

I put the items back in the pack. I stood up and started walking down the trail. It was crude and covered mainly with pine needles. I found myself moving faster and less carefully as I progressed.

How do I get myself in these messes?

After about an hour of walking, I sat down on a large downed pine tree. I pulled out the map and compass. I noticed up ahead not more than a quarter mile, the path bifurcated. I was to take the left hand branch. I would follow that branch approximately a quarter mile reaching a small shack. That's what was circled on the map. That was my objective. I began walking at a very rapid pace.

Not 10 minutes later I found the trail was beginning to wane. I took the left hand turn. I was now jogging at a slow rate of speed. Over my left shoulder I could see the sun slowly fading in the west. Although it was not thick forest, there was enough undergrowth to make me nervous about not reaching the shack by nightfall. I moved down the path approximately 10 more minutes. I could tell the trail was now hit and miss. Then the trail ended totally. There was not a hint of human activity. I scanned the valley below and up the southern ridge I could see nothing that looked like a shack. I pulled the map out of the back pack. I saw a small note on the map.

It said, "Trail End's here." As I looked more closely at the details of the map, I saw a short distance from the end of the walk a note, "old snag". I looked around one more time. And I saw ahead almost due west of my position, an old pine. The top of the dead tree was gone. The base of the tree, I estimated to be at least two feet through.

That must be the one.

The sun had already traversed the ridge of the canyon across from me. I had less than an hour of daylight left. I could feel the cool air begin to move. I headed toward the old snag. My heart was pounding. I sensed fear and excitement both at the same time. I moved rapidly to the dead giant. When I arrived I realized that I had been gradually traversing uphill. I was beginning to feel the presence of someone or something.

I turned around rapidly. I saw nothing. As I walked up to the withering conifer I looked down. There, no more than 100 yards from my position, appeared to be the slats of an old shack. I started scrambling in that direction. Before I knew it, emotion had overtaken me. I was running. Then suddenly I felt a blow to my back. I heard a loud screech and I found myself tumbling to the ground. I felt the backpack nearly ripped from my shoulder. I realized I was being attacked! As I took a step, I lost my footing and began tumbling end for end. I rolled nearly 75 feet. I sprung to my feet and let out what must have been a blood-curdling yell. Then I realized I was face to face with my attacker.

I now recognized a young mountain lion, frozen in place and looking at me with piercing eyes. I searched the ground and was lucky to find a nice sized stone lying right in front of me. I bent down slowly and grabbed the fist sized rock and let it fly right in the direction of the young, 60 to 80 pound cat. It was one of those lucky shots. The rock hit the cat with a thud. Which, even now, I can hear in my mind. The cat turned like lightening and bounded down the hill to the valley floor and disappeared from sight. My heart was pounding so loud that I could hear it in my ears. I was breathless.

"I'm not hurt, I'm not hurt." I said attempting to reassure myself that indeed I was okay. I stood up, checked my damaged knee and found a large abrasion. I could feel blood slip down my back. "I can't let myself get out of control like this in the future," I said limping in the direction of the shack.

The door was open. Wood slats filled the windows. I cautiously made my way inside. I slammed the small midget sized door shut and secured it. I was safe at least for the moment. I looked over to the back wall. Hanging there was a note that said, "Jake". I took the note off the wall. I began reading it.

It simply said, "Proceed 200 yards at a an azimuth 0° due north."

I took a moment to look around the shack. I noticed lying on the floor was a small first aid kit.

I don't have time for this. How were they to know I was going to be mauled by a mountain lion?

I tied my shirt back together as best I could. I put the items that hung out of the large hole in my backpack back in and used the string and needle from the first aid kit to repair the backpack. I left the shack and walked the hundred yards zero degrees north. As I began to pace off the hundred yard distance precisely, I noticed about 100 yards ahead was a small pile of rocks. I went over to the stones and looked down.

The stack was in the form of an arrowhead pointing to west. So I continued in that direction. After about 40 yards I found an out cropping of boulders and as I looked carefully at the wall I noticed a mound of slag that didn't look right. It looked like someone had dumped the earthen material there. So I began to remove the stone slowly. Some were small boulders. I had to use a pry bar to move the last few. Well, not a real one more like a small tree trunk. I could see that the pieces of sandstone concealed an opening. Daylight was just beginning to fade as I crawled into the portal that seemed to expand as I inched forward on hands and knees.

CHAPTER 11

JANUARY 9, 2001, CONTAINED COMMITMENT

Sherry sat in the corner, on a small bench that was made of stone. Around her shoulders was the small blanket she had discovered a few weeks earlier. She reached over and grabbed another handfull of pinion seeds from the large seed bowl she had discovered. The constant drip, drip, drip of the water on the far side of the cave was not even an irritant to her ears. The seasonal water and the nuts were the only things that sustained her life the past few weeks. Her fingers were now testing the limits of her memory in the cave. With her right hand she felt the notches in the Stonewall. Each morning when awakened, she would make a notch in the same place on the wall. These notches she thought represented a day. Today she counted 30. By now the numerous scrapes, scratches and even her broken rib were mostly healed.

Next she began her routines. "Give me strength and help me to be thankful for the life that I have. I would love to get out of here." She prayed.

She began feeling sorry for herself. She knew it was not healthy to dwell in the past but she had so much time on her hands. Why had he left so abruptly and why had he never corresponded, spoken, or even cared that he had hurt her so much? She wondered who ever really knew that she and Jake had spent time together years before.

She remembered the passion they had for each other under the stars, back in the cove, in the rowboat, tied up to a log. She laughed as she saw Jake's face turn so red when Granny told his dad that she had not seen Jake and Sherry earlier that evening. That guy in the red and white converse tennis shoes had put Granny up to it. Sherry breathed a long and slow breath. It seemed so long ago now. She felt good as she thought back over the years of teaching. *The drugs are not going through our campus and the Mexican drug lords will have to find another way to destroy the families of our region.* She thought.

There is no way I would have been hired into the FBI right out of law school without extensive background in martial arts and personal defense. A black belt in jujitsu didn't hurt either. She knew without a doubt, that she had been blessed in so many ways. She slowly moved her hand over the vacant spot that used to brandish the medallion she had left for him; the most important possession she owned. Her mind turned to the task at hand and as usual she offered up a silent prayer. "Our father who art in heaven," she began and then finally she asked for the disciplined thoughts, responses and investments as she continued the most daunting task of her life. Her thoughts turned to her friends.

Why hasn't he come, where is Christian? Memories were now all she had. Memories that would take her away from this place and the pain she felt in her loss.

Jake can't have disappointed me, she thought. While she had cataloged the stories and thought about them from time to time, her new challenges made them live again. She remembered one of the many stories told to her that wonderful summer so many years earlier. She even smiled for a moment as she could hear his talking with excitement in his voice recalling his campfire sagas.

It was these campfire stories, that helped her stay connected to Jake and his family through the years. These memories were now more important than ever. they were all she had, or so she thought. She felt a warmth come over her as she remembered Jake and his ability to handle the school faculty. *Jake learned a lot from the campfire* she sighed.

She crawled slowly to the water that was dripping down and took a long slow drink. As she peered into the pool of water, she began to see the image of a face. While it was totally dark in the cave, Sherry saw light coming out of the water. In the beginning she thought she saw her own face in the water. As time progressed she could tell it was someone or something else.

From the lips of the amorphous face she thought she heard, "What do you really know of love?"

A chill shivered through the whole length of her body. She just sat and looked at the face. The image would stretch and grow tighter as the ripples moved across the surface of the water. After what seemed to be one minute, the image spoke again. "What is love?"

A second set of shivers ran down Sherry's spine.

"Who are you?" she finally demanded."

"I am your comfort, I will protect you. I am Ariel Aion for I am with you forever." The voice said.

"I will comfort and provide hope for you if you ask. Do you trust that I will?"

"I am not sure I really know you, and it's so dark and depressing here." Sherry replied.

"Go to the entrance of the cave. Stand on the far left side. Put your cheek against the wall. Place your hand at eye level. Straight out from your right shoulder you will find a small stone very rough to the touch. Push in on it. Then push it over to the left. Then you find another. Once they are removed, you will then discover inside, the first Kal."

First Kal what is that?

By now she thought she knew every inch of the cell to which she was assigned. Sherry went to the covered opening of the cave that she hopelessly had tried to break through in the past. As she had been instructed she stood on the left side of the cave. She put her hand out, felt for the stone. She focused on the right stone. She discovered one that was different. It was very rough. She pushed hard on the stone. The stone moved out of its place. She pushed it back and to the left as she had been instructed. She then noticed a second stone that was in place behind the first. It was loose. She pulled that stone out. She heard a few more stones fall into the small crevasse she had created. She cleared the stones from the small hole. She had created a tiny tunnel.

The tunnel was a few feet long. She leaned over and pushed her head and shoulders into the opening. She strained her arms and pushed straight ahead. One stone was slightly outside of the others. It was easy to move with a small log used as a pry bar. As she levered it out of place, she heard a boulder slowly grind on the floor below. It was like it rolled backward just a little. As it rolled back it created an even bigger tunnel.

All of a sudden small beams of light flickered across her face.

"It's like the face of an angel," she said out loud.

Behind her she thought she heard, "I am a word with wings," it came from the water.

"Thank you, thank you, thank you," Sherry said. Sherry tried to move more of the large boulders but she could not. The warm stream of light was enough for her. She stood in the light soaking up the heat and gradually opening her eyes. Her vision focused and became clear.

Now that the light began to shine in, she could see more of her cell. She saw the small pool. It was larger than she thought; she could see the seed pot. There was a small pile of wood just out of reach above the bench. The bench had been her bed for the past few weeks. She was thankful. She noticed a small shelf above the bench. On the shelf was a pile of old newspapers she pulled the newspapers down. As a paper fell to the stone floor, she noticed a small book of matches floated to the floor with the paper.

She remembered what now appeared to be a fire spot in a corner. There was an inverted funnel in the ceiling about 20 feet above the small depression. She looked up as she pinched her eyes nearly closed. There was no light coming from the small hole in the center of the funnel. She hoped that it was a vent to the outside. She hurriedly grabbed some of the newspapers and formed the pages into crumpled balls. She put them in the pit and lit them on fire. She, now with the painstaking gate of an 80 year old woman walked back and forth putting small logs on the fire that she had built. The room was filled with smoke. That smell, along with the warmth the fire provided felt good. As the fire radiated its soothing stream she began to feel like life was worth living.

"Thank you Ariel you are an Angel." She said out loud. The little fire became a healing force. After over a month of feeling sorry for herself she sensed hope. She lay down on the bench beside the pit. And slept with a sense of comfort.

CHAPTER 12

JANUARY 10, 2001, ROSETTA STONE

The evening was cool and clear. While the air was dry I could smell the musty humidity inside the cave. I slowly crawled deeper into the stone tunnel. I noticed to the left, in the twilight shadows, a large room. I crawled in and stood up. On the far side of the room sat a pine table and two small chairs.

I walked over and sat down at one of the chairs. In the center of the table I saw a small white envelope resting under an old kerosene lamp. I rotated the lamp just enough to reveal my name on the envelope. I picked it up and opened it. There was a book of matches inside. I took one of the matches and struck the head against the striker. It lit. I put the burning match on the top edge of the wick and watched as the light grew brighter. In the dim flickers, I could see a small bed covered with a large animal skin. In the corner near the entrance I saw a bag of beans. As I turned back to the table I noticed that there was a letter in the envelope from which I had obtained the matches.

I opened the paper and began to Read. "Jake, if you are reading this, congratulations you have managed to locate the start of your journey. If you complete those tasks ahead of you, you will be ready."

"Ready for what?" I asked out loud.

While I didn't expect an answer I almost thought I heard Someone say, "Patience my son, all in good time."

Suddenly I felt frightened, not like a little, but like a lot! I began to realize that I was alone in the middle of the southwestern United States. I noticed that I was cold and that I was shivering. I think I was shivering more from fear than cold.

Why am I fearful? I thought.

Just as I was pondering my circumstance, three individuals each with their face covered and dressed in black, burst into the room. I naturally sprawled onto the floor as the first to reach me knocked me to the ground. As I easily subdued the initial attacker with a hammer lock, the second and third hit me from behind. I resisted the urge to panic. I then did a "sit-out" with my left leg sliding under my right. At the same time I pulled the little finger of one of my assailants. This broke his grip on my waist. As I landed a blow to the collar bone area of one attacker I felt the prick of a needle breaching my skin. I suddenly began to feel my body growing limp. The next thing I recalled was waking up in the bed in the corner of the cave. I noticed the small entry hole was now blocked by a steel plated door. I was imprisoned.

"What's going on here?" I said out loud.

It was at that moment I noticed that my hands were duct taped and that my ankles were likewise secured. I immediately began to bite and tear at the tape with my teeth. Moments later I had my hands and feet free and I sprang to the door. It was secured from the back side. I was still trapped and there was no sign of my assailants. I walked over to the backpack I had left in the corner of the room. It looked as though it had not been disturbed. I took stock of the contents again. As I placed the items on the small table one by one, I stopped for a moment and took a drink from the water bottle. I then took the multi-tool out of the pack and began to survey each of the elements. What I was looking for was a blade or something the might be useful in my escape. As I scanned the cave room in the dim flickering light, provided by the small lamp on the table I noticed that the frame of the small door was wood.

I can use the serrated knife blade to cut through the frame. Slow down, I told myself in my most reassuring thought. *I can't afford any mistakes.*

I reached into the pack and pulled out the now somewhat wrinkled map. I slowly wrote with the small pencil:

"remain calm in all things and trust in your God given gifts."

For a moment I was able to visualize my granddad in an old wood shed on the island. The shed was filled with cedar pieces he used to light the stove in the old white cabin that sat crouched on old cedar logs out over the water. He pulled from his pocket a shiny new Boy Scout knife. I was nine at the time.

He said, "Jake now you can use this as a tool. Be careful the blade is sharp. Let me show you how sharp."

He pulled a piece of cedar measuring one inch by four inches. He pushed down on back side of the open blade against the end of the wood. The blade was sliding with the grain. The wood split easily.

"You try," he said.

I pushed hard on the back of the blade as he watched. Suddenly the blade raced down through the soft cedar like butter. Then he showed me how I could cut through the grain at an angle. "That's how ya whittle," he said with a laugh.

Suddenly it struck me, cut through the frame. By cutting through the frame I could, very possibly, unlatch the door from the outside. I then pulled from the backpack, the small bag of walnuts. As I slowly chomped on the nuts I realized that this entire exercise was nothing more than a test.

This revelation and the food allowed me to slowly construct the resolution that I had been searching for. Now rather than lost and fearful I became stronger in my resolve, not only to escape my current problem but also to help rescue Sherry. In my fear I was only able to think of my own problems and insecurities. Now I was committed to something bigger than me; the mission.

At that moment I thought of what Sherry must be enduring. I stopped in the middle of my thoughts. I did not really want to know what Sherry had to deal with. I took a large swig of water from the jug and walked over to the small door with my multitool. With a small three inch serrated blade, I began the arduous task of cutting through the cedar wood frame. I began making rapid progress in my first cut. Actually, the work became easy. The wood was soft. I finished the first section within five minutes. I started the second cut approximately three inches below the first. In a couple of minutes I was through the wood. Then I banged on the small three by four inch piece. I heard a thud on the far side of the door as the piece I had knocked out hit the ground. "Thanks Gramps," I said with a laugh as I peeked through the hole.

Yes, I thought, *The hole is just large enough for me to stick my arm through.*

I felt around the outside of the door. There was a small latch on the outside. I resisted my anger and searched the outside of the door for the latch. Suddenly I felt the latch on the outside of the door unlock as I worked blindly at the piece of metal.

What do you do once you are outside of the door I wondered? Slowly I pushed the door open. I crawled outside the door.

"Remember to the right is freedom," I said to myself quietly.

To the left was in the unknown. I chose to go to the left. I crawled about 10 feet. I came to a door on my right. The door was similar to the one I had just exited. As I entered the room, I was struck by how large the room was. Kerosene lights were already illuminating the room. At the nearest wall ahead of me and behind a very large table hung some sort of skin, possibly deer hide, with painted pictures on it.

Next to the hide stood two humans dressed in black. One of the figures' arms slowly, slowly pointed out elements on the hide.

Why don't you just talk to me? This is a map of this cave castle.

CHAPTER 13

January 10, 2001, The Story

Clouds totally obscured the sun. A slow steady drizzle filtered down adding additional dampness to the already heavy, depressing air. Inside the court house things were not much different. At precisely 10:00 AM Wednesday January 10th, 2001 the court was called to order by the honorable Dustin J. Blice. It seemed to juror number nine; a 64 year old white male, like an endless litany of instructions. There were instructions to the members of the press, the spectators, the jury, the defense team and the prosecution. Finally Judge Blice said to the prosecutor, "madam you may proceed."

"Your Honor the prosecution calls Mr. Ieke Rollands to the stand and we request that he be treated as a hostile witness. He has been uncooperative to this point."

The prosecutor asked Mr. Rollands all the basic questions.

"Please state your name and spell it for the record"

"I am Ieke Rollands spelled: I e k e R o l l a n d s."

"Who is your employer?"

"I run the Seattle Public School system; I mean I work for the Seattle School Board of Directors."

"Is that a big job?"

"Well we serve forty five thousand students and our annual budget is half a billion dollars. What do you think?" Rollands asked with a smile and a twinkle in his eye.

"How much of that budget is federal money?" The prosecutor asked.

"Objection your honor, relevance," Mr. Cage said.

"Sustained," Blice said.

"Your Honor," the tall brunette prosecutor started.

"I know, I will take it under advisement and we can come back to it later." Blice interrupted.

"Proceed," Blice said.

"Where were you on the morning of November 10, 2000 at approximately 9:00 AM?"

"I was jogging on the Seattle waterfront."

"Is that in King County?"

"Yes it is."

"What did you see on the morning of November 10, when you were out on your jog?"

"Well I saw two men floating in the harbor off pier 56 on what I thought was a raft of logs."

"Was that odd to you that two men would be floating on a raft of logs?"

"Most definitely."

"So you contacted the police?"

"Objection Your Honor the prosecutor is leading the witness," the defense attorney said.

"Sustained," Judge Blice said in an almost sarcastic tone.

"I'll rephrase your honor, "What did you do next?"

"I continued jogging."

"Did you describe what you saw to anyone?"

KNIGHT JUSTICE

"Who did you contact?" The prosecutor continued.

"The police,"Rollands replied.

"So you called the police, is that correct?"

"That's what I told you."

"So your answer to my question is yes, is that correct?"

Snickers were heard throughout the gallery.

"Why sir, did you contact the police?" queried the prosecutor.

"Because I thought it odd for two men to be floating in the harbor taped to a log raft." Rollands responded.

Robust laughter erupted from the spectators.

"Order, I will have order in this court," Judge Blice growled.

"What did you tell the police?"

"I told them two men were in the harbor floating on a raft."

"After contacting the police what did you do next?" the prosecutor asked.

Rollands responded, "I continued on with my jog."

"No further questions," the tall dark haired female said.

Judge Blice then called the defense attorney Mr. Cage.

"Have you any questions?" He inquired.

As he made his way to the front of the desk the, defense attorney said, "We do Your Honor."

"Mr. Rollands," Do you know this man," the attorney for Carlos asked as he pointed towards Carlos.

Ieke Rollands paused for a moment and then replied, "He is not a friend, if that is what you are asking."

"That is not what I asked." The attorney fired back.

"Is it true that on Nov 10, 2000 you and Carlos Castilano, the defendant, were at least acquaintances prior to the report that you saw the two people floating on the raft which you have testified that you believed odd?"

There were a few snickers from the gallery.

After a long pause Rollands replied, "That depends on the definition of acquaintance."

"Your Honor," The Prosecutor chimed in, "Are we on a fishing expedition?"

Judge Blice replied, "Please define for Mr. Rollands the word acquaintance."

Mr. Cage replied, "Mr. Rollands, as I am sure you are aware an acquaintance is someone you know at least slightly."

The attorney then asked, "Mr. Rollands, did you slightly know Mr. Castilano before the report of the raft?"

Rollands, "yes."

The defense attorney asked, "Did you ever speak to or in any way have contact with Mr. Castilano prior to the raft report?"

Rollands said, "but we are not friends if that is what you are driving at."

"Would a copy of your phone records help your memory?" the attorney asked.

"Objection, Mr. Rolland's is not on trial here," the prosecutor said.

"There has been no foundation Your Honor."

"Sustained, "Judge Blice responded.

"Strike the question Your Honor," The defense attorney said.

"No further questions at this time." Cage ended.

Judge Blice said, "If the state has no further questions." He paused, then pounded his gavel on the desk top and said, "It is now 11:48 AM we will recess until 1:30 PM."

The judge said, "I will see both prosecutor and defense in my office." He left the room.

CHAPTER 14

THAT SAME MORNING, JAVA JIVE

In a small coffee shop a few blocks from the courthouse sat three people dressed in shabby slacks and wrinkled shirts. They looked like custodians at the end of a shift. They sat discussing final plans. The woman, tallest of the three asked, "Did either of you have any problems getting into the court house earlier this morning?"

The others looking at each other indicated that they had not.

"I just received a message from the big man and he says court has just been dismissed until 1:30 PM. We have a few minutes to go over final details. There should be no problem getting back into the court. In your back packs you have a package of brand new Bic pens. What do we do as soon as we get to the court conference room?"

"We take the pens apart and place the points in the plastic cones. Then we tape them onto the small hole at the small end of the cone. Then we superglue the cones to the lip of the aluminum coffee cup just around the sip hole." the skinny guy said.

"Correct," the woman said, "and make sure you glue the sip hole closed. Do you both have the glue?"

"I have mine." The Skinny guy said.

The chubby fellow just nodded and grunted.

"Remember you will only have a few seconds to place the cup on the windowsill before the fireworks start. I will bring the dry ice and hot water in a waste paper container through the judge's entrance to the court room. I noticed that Blice has a heater behind his desk. It will work well in distributing the CO_2 gas. Make sure the police are out of the way. I will stop by the conference room and provide you with the dry ice for your coffee after he finishes his testimony. We had better head back to the court."

The three walked out each carrying a small pack loaded with tape, pens, quart sized coffee cups and superglue. Each carried a small, plastic, one inch long tube that looked like two funnels attached together at the small end. Together these items were the simple components that would make up their dry ice blasters.

CHAPTER 15

January 10, 2001, Trainee Trainer

was totally unaware of what was going on outside. I was now focused on the happenings of the cave and my own experiences. While the entire setting freaked me out to say the least, I was drawn to the crude map and the information on it. After escaping from my little cave like cell I, through my own choice, found myself. Yes my own choice. Yes I could have turned to the right. Instead I turned to the left. Yes I could have been dreaming but for me the chance for adventure drew me in.

My attention was on the hand painted hide map. I was specifically noting the details of the scale drawn on the bottom right hand corner. It said five centimeters equals 100 kilometers. At that very moment I realized that on the surface of the map were descriptions of an immense system of underground tunnels, as well as large and small caves. The system must have been hundreds of miles in length.

This maze of underground tunnels and caves covered what I estimated to be portions of the states of New Mexico and Colorado. In fact I thought I saw a section that ran into lower Utah and some of area 51 in Nevada. I was familiar with area 51 because I had read the strange and sometimes unbelievable tales.

Most of the underground passages were connected. Like a vast underground highway system. At the top left corner of the map there was a huge section, dull red in color. Area 51 was stenciled right in the middle; the site of the mystery and rumors of UFO's and strange activity. I remembered seeing a story of a huge craft that had "anti-gravity engines," and made of materials not of our world.

Lightly dotted black lines marked what I assumed to be state borders. I also thought I saw a notation for Colorado Springs. It said CS but was just east of a mountain PP which I thought must be Pikes Peak. Colorado Springs is the region where several underground military installations are located. It seemed logical that there might be caves in that area. Yet it was a stretch to think that there was a network of caves throughout the southwestern United States. It was hard to fathom a network as vast as it appeared on the map.

Much of it referenced gold and silver mines that peppered Colorado in the 1800's. I noticed Silverton and Carlsbad Caverns but there were more. Many more! I recalled the uranium, coal and other mineral mines in the area and wondered if this map might somehow be related. I knew about Roswell and all the intrigue around it. But why were these men introducing me to the map?

Do they think Sherry is hidden in one of these networks? I must be dreaming this is just too unreal.

One thing I knew, I was in a cave and I was responsible for committing the map to memory. I had been told that was my task. Dreaming or not I had to remember the details. I studied the structure of the map. I especially focused on what I believed to be each city notation in close proximity to many of the tunnel locations.

Christian's words rang in my ears. "You must learn to recall the details or you will never be able to help save Sherry."

Fantasy or not, I knew that the details of every experience from this moment on would be of potential value.

The black clothed freaky figure continued to point out various locations as I asked questions. From time to time, as I asked questions, I thought I detected movement from behind me. I would flinch and then turn to what seemed to be nothing, nothing but a very dark cave. When I asked questions with a who or why contained in the body, I received nothing but stone cold indifference. Yet, when I asked for a location like "Where is Denver," the ninja like figure would point to map.

I asked for example, "where is Lechuguilla Cave?" I was directed to a region over 100 miles long in the Carlsbad park area.

I asked, "Where is the area 51 to Roswell tunnel?" I asked that question because I wanted to know if the two locations were really connected. According to some folks there is a vast system of tunnels and caves that supposedly have been developed under the areas of Native American and nationally owned grounds. Some have even suggested that there are "underground cities". These housed more than just military installations if the popular cult writing was to be believed. Supposedly these subterranean cities contain treasures and secrets with extraordinary implications. Anyway, I was surprised when I got the response to my question.

I was shown a dark red line represented hundreds of miles. I remembered the words, "you see it, but it is not there!"

These words were right under the red line.

This is wild.

Yet I was not totally surprised because I had read of the discovery and mining of uranium on the Navaho lands. I had also seen pictures of the massive underground drills that can tunnel through solid rock at a rate of more than a few miles a day. I hoped that I would be able to recall the specifics of the map because for me this level of knowledge was in a strange way captivating. I knew it had to be related to the abduction of Sherry. Dang it all, what I knew of the underground accommodations right where I was standing made me a believer.

The map indicated that the system in which we were housed seemed to be part of a smaller network associated with, but not totally integrated into the other areas I had just seen.

Then I asked, "Where is Christian right now?"

I was surprised that the figure pointed to what I knew to be the same location as I.

Is Christian one of these strange black clothed people? Duly noted, at least he has to be very near me! That was if all the spooky stuff could be believed.

Each and every time the spooky ghost like person pointed out a location on the map in a direct response to a where question I asked.

So, why not ask it? Finally I just blurted it out. "Where is Sherry now?" I asked.

To my surprise and utter astonishment the figure pointed to a small cave some distance from my location. The distance, it seemed to me, was no more than 50 miles. I looked closely and saw that the position I thought might be Sherry's prison was not directly connected to the system I was now in. In other words Sherry was very possibly in a cave not that far from my current one. Her prison was in a different, adjacent system. The map just was not that precise. That is if I could trust what I was seeing in the first place.

As I continued to cram as many facts I learned from the map as I could into my memory banks, I was unnerved. This time, somehow, I detected a presence behind me. I spun around just as two black clothed individuals rushed me. This time I was ready.

I fell back as the first person reached towards me. As I did, I extended my right leg outward catching the assailant in the chest as I rolled back. The blow flung the attacker over the top of me and into

KNIGHT JUSTICE

the table next to the map. The one who had been at the map made a rush in my direction. My focus then turned to the other attacker who was coming at me. I grabbed a foot and twisted lifting up rapidly. This quick and forceful move spun the attacker away from me and into the solid rock of the cave wall. As I scrambled to my feet I saw the entrance to the room. I ran turning to the right and into complete darkness. I knew from an inset on the map that there was another room not more than 50 yards down the black tunnel ahead.

I visualized the expanded insert on the map as I moved forward into the darkness. According to the map, the tunnel I was now moving slowly down, led to a room labeled on the upper section of the map as MR. As I stumbled along the cold dark corridor, I kept my right hand against the wall. In this way I could keep my balance and also I should know when I hit the opening to the room. As I continued on, I saw a small speck of light leaking out from under the door on my right.

An instant later I burst into the large chamber. Craning my head around, to make sure that I was not being overtaken by the black masked marauders I was stunned by a bright light. The light must have been motion activated. As I looked back in the direction of the room I noticed Christian and three others sitting at a table. Furious, I lunged towards Christian who was seated across a large table from me.

"Good to see you," Christian said slowly, "Congratulations you have made it to the final stage of your training."

"Scourges!" I yelled at the top of my lungs.

CHAPTER 16

JANUARY 9, 2001, LIFE CHECK

A small ray of sunlight shone brightly through the tiny hole in the rock filled opening in the cave. This light warming her closed eyelids reminded Sherry that a new day was dawning. Still very weak and groggy, she awakened to the sounds of fading cracks and pops. The noise came from the dying embers of the small fire she had built the night before.

Not very many days earlier, she had been freed from darkness by the instructions she had followed from her water-encased friend. Sherry was pondering what Ariel had last said to her as she slowly faded back into the water. When Sherry last saw Ariel, she heard her say, "To Israel is to follow the lion."

Sherry heard herself mumbling "To Israel is to follow, to Israel is to follow, to Israel is to follow the lion." Sherry felt she really needed an even closer connection with Ariel Aion now. In reality they had bonded. She was still baffled and frustrated by the words Ariel spoke. She looked forward to seeing and hearing from Ariel, yet she could not unwrap the meaning. She felt herself biting down on her lower lip as she was becoming more frustrated. She was now fully awake.

"Ariel, are you there?"

The name Ariel, to Sherry was becoming the enduring power of hope. Ariel not only helped Sherry feel the embrace that hope provided; she was feeling a connection so real that she was for Sherry nothing less than the essence of hope. She was the substance and the evidence all wrapped together. Sherry had seen Ariel and heard from her in the small pool of water when She needed a friend. Ariel could be counted on and relied upon. It went farther than friendship. Ariel was what Sherry was clinging to. By following the specific directions she had heard from Ariel, Sherry pulled a rock free from the sealed entrance. That act of trust was more precious than gold to Sherry.

Once she freed the rock from its resting place, a small beam of light was instantly visible, her only contact with the outside. As Sherry reflected on the experience she grew warmer from the inside out like a warm drink of tea. She now had fire and light which had eluded her for so many weeks. For Sherry the drive to survive was stronger than ever. This discovery of light was seemingly so small, and yet really her source of increasing hopes.

Sherry walked rather than slide along the cold rocky floor. She now slept through the night because she was warmed by the fire she was so careful to nurture. She now had a set of routines. The routines were simple. Wake up, place a small log on the coals and blow softly until a small flame would emerge. Eat a small handful of the precious nuts from the burlap sack and drink from the water of the small pool.

She was careful not to eat more than two handfuls of pinion nuts a day and she calculated she could last 40 more days. As for the logs, she counted the pile and found that it contained 150 individual pieces of wood. If she used not more than three a day she could last until the warm days of spring. She was sure that by the time the sun would be warming the earth each spring day, she would be rescued from her cell in the cave.

In addition to her meager day to day existence, Sherry now carved out for herself a stronger and more trusting relationship with Ariel. By now she had abandoned any concern that she might have lost her mind. She simply didn't care. This angel of the words was her companion. While she longed for and wanted the touch of a human more than ever, she was willing to accept her plight. Ariel spoke with and comforted her.

By providing words of wisdom, information and encouragement she gave Sherry courage and strength. Most importantly, Ariel Aion was now a prime life force. Sherry was glad to be alive in no small part due to Ariel's gestures of love and support. At the same time, the life form in the water, gave Sherry the perspective and guidance she so greatly needed. This allowed her to endure.

As Sherry finished her daily routines she heard Ariel again. She was responding directly to Sherry's inability to unravel the meaning.

"Why are you here?" the voice rang out from the darkness just below the surface of the water in a now familiar tone. Sherry sat for a moment before responding.

"I don't even know where I am and I have no good reason to right now."

"I will tell you directly, you are in Gullahgilgalel because of para-koe," said the watery image.

"Am I supposed to sit here until I have it all figured out? I just start to get one thing you tell me and then you give me more," Sherry complained.

"You will know as you trust. As you drink my water and walk my ground you grow strong in the hupakoe."

"Am I just to trust you, an image and a voice in the water?"

"Always know there is help." The voice retorted.

"I can't even help myself and from here I sure can't help you."

"What about others?"

The vale of clouds was beginning to clear for Sherry. She was seeing in her essence what was important. *Why yes*, Sherry recalled, *just think of the kids I saved from the slave traders as well as the drug gangs that I broke up. That's not to mention the latest attempt by Carlos, Razier and the others to take money from the school funding system which was intended to help children. Education is a nearly a trillion dollar industry and the national funding component alone is worth billions. I helped stop that attempt or at least I hope I did.*

"I tried." Sherry responded with her tongue thrusting staccato into her words.

"But was it important?"

"Yes to me and my friends."

"But who are your friends and who can you trust for the good shama?" The voice roared like waves from the ocean.

"Well there is Jake, I know I can trust him: Then there is Chris he would always do the right; Ieke Rollands is helpful…" Sherry said with increasingly less confidence.

"Beware," Ariel said, "traitors are amongst the good and liars injure the all."

"Are you suggesting that I can't even trust my friends?"

"Know this: you can trust but one and all others will disappoint!"

"Shama the one and you will be safe, but trust only the one!" Ariel then faded slowly into the darkened surface of the pool and was gone. Sherry sat for a moment and wondered what Ariel meant, "Trust only one."

If I trust only one, then all others will disappoint. How can I not trust those in the Knights of St. John?

CHAPTER 17

JANUARY 9, 2001, CLEAR CRYSTAL

The light in the room was still glaring in my eyes. I was squinting at those sitting before me.

"Sit down at our table," Christian said with a smile. "Please call me Chris!"

While I heard what he said, the long scramble down the pitch dark hall was still affecting my ability to see. In a similar way, my mind was scrambling to guide me towards the proper response. I figured the challenges of the past few days had been part of my training but I was not totally sure.

Why trap me in a small room and attack me for no reason? I wondered.

Were these ninja people I had just eluded playing a cruel joke on a willing dupe or was I really being tested? Regardless, I was not amused, nor was I in a mood to be sitting. My heart was pounding so loudly in my temples that I could scarcely hear anything else. I noticed that I was shaking uncontrollably. I decided to walk. I paced slowly from one end of the table to the other. I turned to the open stone arched door a few times as I was sure

KNIGHT JUSTICE

my attackers were about to lunge through it at any moment. After what might have been 30 seconds I noticed that there was food and lots of it spread around the large flagstone table. Since I had not eaten anything substantial for days I could not help but reconsider Chris's offer.

"You people have some explaining to do," I blurted out.

Chris looked me straight in the eye and said calmly, "What would you like to know?"

"For starters," I said, "did you know I was attacked by a mountain lion and roughed up by creeps dressed in black?"

"Well, yes I guess I did," Chris replied. "You were filmed by our cameras every step of the way. Would you like to watch and learn?"

I had heard those exact words, "would you like to watch and learn," from Chris before. I have to admit that when he asked if I wanted to watch and learn, generally I did much more learning then watching. In my previous experiences I would be given a task then I was filmed doing whatever it was. I would then be put through hours of training by experts on how I might be more effective. This would go on until I could do what I was asked perfectly. I was now beginning to understand. So if I had not learned from these experiences I might be challenged to repeat some of them. In the meantime the food on the table looked quite good.

So after a long pause I said, "I could sure use a few bites of that roast turkey right now."

Chris smiled and asked. "Have you washed up?"

I rubbed my hands vigorously on my thighs and pulled out one of the large mansanita wood chairs and sat down. I noticed that the entire stone topped table was supported by what appeared to be three large mansanita stumps, each at least a foot in diameter.

"Where did you ever find this fine furniture?" I questioned the third man sitting at the far end of the table.

The man with leathery dark skin, peering over his black glass-es replied, "This furniture has been in here, in this underground complex for at least 300 years and was carried by my ancestors from Mexico during the great rebellion of 1680 against the Spanish." He was small in stature and had flowing, almost white hair.

"So, do you have Ohkay Owingeh or Santa Clara in your back-ground?" I asked seriously.

"You know your history, my son," he said slowly. "I am of the clan of Tewa and now live on the first mesa but I am a descendent of the great leader Po'pay."

"So what brings you here?" I queried softly.

"You are on my ancient fathers' ground and we must learn to-gether the meaning of your experiences. My friend Chris is here to guide us. You wear around your neck an ancient Clovis point given to you by your sister Sherry Paul. What you do not know: my people of the Hopi-Tewa, many, many moons ago lived in the great moun-tains of Montana and Idaho and even into Spokane and the great hills of the Okanagan. Ever since my people lived in peace with the Spaniards we have shared a common purpose with the Knights of St. John.

Are you aware that the Ohkay Owingeh was once called San Juan? It was named for St. John the Baptist, the saint of the Knights. My people gave the point you now wear to the great leader of the Okanagan. There has been a special bond of brothers and sisters of the Kiowa of Oklahoma and the Kewa and the Okanagan. Now, my friend, you are about to be joined into that same community. Are you ready and willing to be a brother with us?"

"Can I eat first?" I said with a chuckle.

"Never forget to laugh my friend," the Old Man said. I liked the Old Man from the moment I set eyes on him. I could tell from the deep etched lines in his face that he was a man of action.

Those were not the lines of age alone. They were forged by years of stress and strain.

Chris slid the large platter of turkey over to me and I grabbed the leg and started eating. It tasted so good that I almost grabbed the other. I then realized that I was not in control. I had given into my own desires. Chris and the Old Man just smiled and watched as I finished the plate in front of me.

"Who are the black ninjas that attacked me?"

Chris scratched his head as he replied, "Who they are, is unimportant. What do they represent, is the question."

I thought for a good minute it seemed. Then I said, "Well I guess they might be my own baggage or the things that weigh me down."

"What might those things be?" The Old Man asked scratching his chin, which was slightly hidden under a sparse, short white beard.

"You know I handled them much better when I was not fearful. In fact the same could be said for the mountain lion. I got in trouble when I got scared. By the way did you guys have anything to do with the lion?" I quizzed.

"Oh, you mean Gil here!" Chris chuckled as the small eighty pound cat jumped out from under the table and stood looking at me.

"Yeah her," I said indignantly. "She tore my backpack."

"Tomorrow we will give you more answers. But for now I think you would like a nice rest." Chris said.

He got up from the table and waived his hand in the direction of the hall bidding me to follow. We exited the room and walked through a small door on the other side of the dark passage into a nicely appointed room with a sink, a bed in the corner and a small lamp on a night stand.

Chris said, "I think you will be comfortable here."

He left the room closing the pine door behind him. I looked at the bed and walked over, took off my well-worn shoes and laid down.

CHAPTER 18

JANUARY 11, 2001, FINAL ORDERS

Kareem Razier was sitting next to the rain spotted window in the small rented apartment just two blocks off East 7th Street in downtown Durango Colorado. His eyes wandered back and forth from the wind weathered oak in the front yard to the TV. He listened more carefully as cable news reporter Fred Fille reviewed the facts surrounding the attack on the USS Cole. The skeleton of the once great Navy ship was resting in Pascagoula, Mississippi. We got you good he muttered as the report of the investigation's progress droned on in the background. It was 9:09 AM. He refocused his attention as the phone rang. Kareem walked slowly over the slanted creaky pine floor and picked up the phone.

"Ya," he said, attempting to send the message to the person on the other end that he was the man in charge. The voice on the other end became louder and lower. The intent was to let Kareem Razier know that he, not Razier was, in charge.

"It is time!" The voice said without a pause.

Kareem Razier replied, "will do."

As he paused for a moment, Kareem heard a click and then nothing but the buzz of a dead connection. He put the receiver down onto

KNIGHT JUSTICE

the holder making sure that the clear plastic switch was depressed. For a moment he reflected on what he was about to do.

To kill her is not easy, no matter how justified I am, he thought as he walked over to the other side of the dingy apartment.

"She deserves to die," he said as he sat down, hoping this vocalization might somehow absolve him of the guilt and anxiety now coming to a boil. He had just been ordered to do what he now was in fear of doing.

Isn't it always the way that the little guys like me are stuck with the messy stuff while the hot shots sit back in their waterfront apartments never having to get dirty hands, he complained to himself.

As he sat on the edge of the bed, he began to rehearse the critical elements of the act. He would make his way to the cave, take the severely weakened and nearly dead Sherry Paul by the hair and yank her as she struggled weakly in vain. He would have timed the events so that, just as the last glimmers of the winter's sun light faded from view it would be done. Finally he would lead Sherry to the edge of the canyon wall and simply shove the woman over the edge. She would have no chance. Especially in her weakened condition.

In the meantime he would have to make at least three or four test runs down the uneven path just to make sure there were no mistakes. *One week is a long time when planning a murder,* he thought as he walked to a small restaurant inside the Strater Hotel just a few blocks from his apartment. In his hand he carried a small black canvas bag which contained a small notebook, four, yellow, number two pencils, and a topographical map of Mesa Verde National Park. He walked over to the first table on the right at the top of the stairs just past the 1950's vintage phone booth complete with a black phone with white numbers under the black dial.

"Hey Mr. R," the young blond waitress said.

"How are you toots?" Razier replied, "I'll have the usual."

85

CHAPTER 19

JANUARY 11, 2001, LAST CHANCE

I was awakened to the buzz of an alarm clock flashing 6:00 AM. A bright sun light was peeking through a small crack in the heavy tartan fabric of the maroon and blue shades. As was my normal practice I hit the snooze button for the last few minutes of blissful repose as I gradually became more and more aware of my surroundings.

I had been so exhausted the night before I barely took note. I saw that I was in a large king size bed in a room that was at least twenty by twenty. The room was nicely appointed. It was furnished of natural woods, probably cedar of some sort. A variety of fabrics including wool and silk were evident. A large desk sat in the corner and a couch lounged in front of a large wood burning fire place. The log was already crackling and popping even at this early hour. Just for a moment I wondered how I ended up here in this nice five star rustic room? Then reality struck.

This was the day I was to receive my final instructions and then I might, depending on how well I performed, be welcomed into the Order. This recollection provided me with the motivation to literally jump out of the bed. As I sprang forward, my mind began to whirl.

I now was reminding myself that in a few short minutes I would be given the background and information I needed to be part of a rescue attempt. Sherry Paul my on again off again friend from childhood was held captive by people I did not really know or really understand. I was in the hands of people I did not trust and did not really like all that much. After all this Christian Poincy and his minions were the only link between me and Sherry.

As for Sherry, I still did not fully understand why and how she had been able to turn my life upside down with not much more than a kiss. None the less I was smitten and head over tea kettle in love with her. At least that was the only explanation I could come up with at the time. Only a few months earlier she had stormed back into my life and grabbed my heart and she took it with her. Somehow deep down I knew I had to follow her and continue the relationship we had for a brief yet wonderful few days.

Walking out of the stone floored shower I wondered, *are we going to find her before it's too late and will she ever be the same?* She was constantly on my mind and I found that I had to force myself to do anything but think of her. Was she alright? Had she been beaten? Had she provided information to her captors? I realized that the never ending stream of questions was not in any way helping to get her back. Yet a good solid plan might help. I got dressed and prepared to do a bit of homework.

As I sat at the large wood and leather desk I was abruptly interrupted when the old Native American I had met for the first time the evening before walked into the room with a tray of fruit, walnuts, cheese, eggs and dark bread. He placed it on the desk.

"It is now 6:45 AM. We will see you across the hall in fifteen minutes." He turned and walked towards the door.

I said with a smile, "Just a minute, don't I get an agenda or something?"

He stopped, turned slowly around and said, "Enough is all you need."

As the door closed slowly behind him I wondered what enough really was. As I scanned the journal I kept of the challenges I had endured for many weeks, I could not help but reflect on the words of the Old Man, "Enough is all you need." *What did he mean?*

I sat down and started to nibble at the breakfast that had been prepared for me. It was all I could do to swallow a few bites of banana, a little cheese, and some walnuts. I chugged down the apple juice. I picked at the poached egg. As I sipped the coffee I leaned back in my chair and thought about my experiences the past five or six week weeks.

There had been so many times that I wanted to quit during the hand to hand combat training and the isolation in the woods, I had nearly walked away. Each and every time I wanted to get out, I did not quit, I just hung in there long enough. *Is that what the Old Man meant? Just do my best; that is all that I can do.* I pushed the tray of food away, finished my note taking and headed out the door. I walked across the hallway that looked and felt like what I believed a Medieval castle might look and feel.

As I opened the huge solid wood door, I saw the same table at which I had eaten and talked the night before. Now the table was full of men of all ages. At the far end of the table was a lone chair. I assumed it to be mine. As I headed in the direction of the last chair I heard Chris's very familiar voice say, "have a seat at the end of the table." I reached the chair and sat down. Then it began.

Chris started with the first question, "please tell us why you are here?" He said.

I paused for an instant then spoke, "I am here because I want to be a Knight of Saint John and I want to find Sherry Paul."

KNIGHT JUSTICE

I noticed that everyone at the table was dressed in a black hooded robe with a white cross on a red background on each chest. Just as I surveyed the group, the old Native American I had by now felt some attachment to said, "Have you any questions of us?"

"Yes I do," I responded promptly. "Who are you really and why are you here?" I asked directly.

A small man at the end of the table said, "Let me begin. I know you are aware of the Knights of St. John from a historical perspective, correct?"

I nodded my head. "Did you know that the French invaded and eventually dispelled the Knights of Saint John from the islands of Malta because the Knight's had become soft and undisciplined?"

"No I did not know that. I thought Napoleon invaded because he was bent on world domination and Malta was a convenient stop." I said.

"Well the truth is that the Knights suffered from poor leadership and bad morale after centuries of leisure."

"Bonaparte reasoned that the only way to save the Knights in 1798 was to destroy them. What the history books will not tell you is that during the 36 hour siege of Malta in early June a few Knights of Saint John were taken prisoner after valiantly defending a small village north of the city of Valletta. The Knights of the Langue of Auvergne fought desperately along with a small but brave group of Christian Maltese peasants whom were eventually captured and taken to Napoleon himself." the small man concluded.

"That is where my great, great grandfather came in," a large, maybe six feet-six inches tall man said.

"Jean why don't you tell us," Chris asked.

"Well it was like this," Jean continued, "Grandpa and nine other friends were fighting along with two Knights on a small flat not too far from where St. Elmo stands today. All Grandpa and the Knights had left were swords and they came upon a group of French regulars, just as the sun was setting. Using the sun's glare to their advantage, the small group rushed straight forward catching the regular Frenchmen without loaded muskets. The Knights swiftly and without mercy beheaded four French and the Maltese made short work of twelve or so others. The remaining French fled back toward the small landing ship from which they had recently embarked. They were also cut down before they could retreat."

"Quickly," the Knight said. "Then the small group put on French uniforms and left the intact bodies in peasant clothing on the road. Clamoring aboard the small landing craft they made a line for L'Orient herself.

Upon coming along side, Clayton De Berry the knight from Auvergne yelled to the officer of the deck in French, 'please escort me and those with me to the Commander-in-Chief take us to Commander Bonaparte.'

To the surprise of all on the tiny little vessel, moments later Napoleon himself emerged from his quarters, walked across the deck and waived his hand allowing the party to board one of the largest vessels in the world. Bonaparte, to the astonishment of my grandfather, gave orders to a French engineer and to Clayton De Berry that they would, command one of his frigates supplying as much of the gold and silver plate that was to be confiscated from the Knights over the following few days and make way to the Americas. So while it is true that much of what was seized from the Knights was loaded on board the pride of the French Navy L'Orient largest vessel in the French fleet. That which was eventually lost was only a portion of the total. The remaining treasure ended up in the Americas."

KNIGHT JUSTICE

"My grandfather was a big part of all this. He delivered in this document what is the rest of the story." Jean waived the actual document in my direction. He paused for a moment and shared with me all the words written in the vellum document.

There on the bottom was the statement:

"I declare in this secret order and so swear, under penalty of death, under the terms of surrender, I hereby appoint Clayton De Berry, Knight of Auvergne as Grand Master of the Knights of St. John and it is he who will set up in the new world a stronghold from which the military arm of the Knights will operate in defense of the ill and the poor whenever and wherever it may be necessary. Not one word of this will be shared without proper authority."
Signed,
Fra Ferdinand von Homspech
Affirmed,
Napoleon Bonaparte Commander-in Chief June 14, 1798.

The large man continued to address me and the others. "Not all the rare treasure of the Knights of St. John supposedly loaded on L' Orient went down in Abukir Bay as history states. Much came to America with my great, great, granddad and two Knights of St. John as well as some French and a small group of loyal Christian Maltese peasants. They landed in central Mexico and eventually came to New Mexico after a long and difficult journey across Texas. The room in which you are now seated was the first headquarters established by the new order in the fall of 1802. If you want to check out the facts you might be interested to know that during the period of time covered by this document there was no real Grand Master only a 'defacto'."

I was stunned and overwhelmed at the same time. If that could have happened then what I was now experiencing could also be real. I was speaking at a table with a leadership group of what is the lost military order of the Knights of St. John.

I sat for what seemed to me to be an eternity then, after shaking my head slowly I asked "Why then is this not public?"

Chris piped up, "Do you really think that we could accomplish all that we have if we were subject to the bickering and indecision of corrupt governments?"

I looked around the huge manzinita table with its massive spiraling legs and darkened and cracked surfaces and each and every person, maybe twenty in all, was nodding in agreement.

For the first time in my life I am in a group that totally believes in each other as well as the mission to serve, to protect and to minister.

"So how many are there of you?" I quizzed.

"You ask a question to which there is no simple response. I will give you my best general synopsis. There are, we believe to be, forty thousand dedicated to the cause. The cause includes the Hospital, feeding of the poor and other service elements. You may know that at the turn of the 19th Century the order was in shambles, many Knights had become undisciplined and directionless. After the loss of Malta the order was like a fatherless child wandering with no sense of purpose or direction.

The good news is that during this time many of the riffs between Catholic, Copt, Protestant, Greek and Russian langues were mended. By the time the Romans reestablished a connection with the Order, the English, Russians and others did also. We as the hidden new American Knights of St. John were busy assisting the Americans in the freedom quest of the early 1800's." Chris concluded.

KNIGHT JUSTICE

Responding to what he had said I asked "So Chris, are you telling me that I am now being considered to join an Order of Knights that by all accounts does not exist?"

"You can be sure we exist," a large man at the far end of the table replied.

"Well are you connected to Nazis or Klu Klux Klan?" I asked.

Chris replied strongly, "You could not be farther from the truth!"

"As for the Nazis," the old Native American continued, "they are Socialists and we believe in free markets and human dignity. They prey on the defenseless. We always oppose those who want to prey on the weak and defenseless."

"We have always fought for freedom and fairness and in fact we spent a considerable amount of our fortune to free slaves in the 1800s and to assist the freedom tours in the South in the 1960's."

"So where do we go from here," I asked.

CHAPTER 20

January 11, 2000, Weak Waiting

The day was cold, even for January, and the wind howled through the small opening in the tunnel. It made a high pitched whistling sound as it entered the cave. Sherry was sitting close to the small and flickering fire in her now well practiced hunch back position. She looked over at the pile of rocks she managed to move out of the small tunnel. The pile was now covering nearly one full corner of the cave in which she sat. She had moved all she could. The large boulders still blocked any hope of climbing to freedom's light. The bright sun was now coming through the cave, more than ever. She however was struggling, she was weak and suffering from what was a constant cough.

It has to be pneumonia, she thought, as she finished a coughing spell that lasted at least five minutes. She sat there with rounded shoulders. Then what was becoming a regular occurrence; she saw flickers in the water. She watched the white bubbles turn to a fog. The fog began to form a shape as the rustling sound that so often singled the appearance of Ariel once again captured Sherry's attention.

"In whom do you put your faith?" The voice rang out from the water.

Sherry with a hoarse almost raspy voice responded, "I have my doubts."

"Everyone has doubts," The voice answered, "why should you feel like you are the Lone Ranger?"

"Yes but I now question everything."

"It is okay to question, but then again, have you found answers?"

"I don't know and maybe don't care," Sherry spoke putting all her force behind her words.

"It is not all right to give in," the voice retorted, "hope is what drives you, not despair."

"Do you still believe in me?"

"Of course I do." Sherry said.

"There is one other you can trust," said the voice.

"Where, who, how?" Sherry asked slowly.

"You can handle this too," the voice said as its visage slowly faded back into the pool.

As Sherry sat on the cold stone bench in the darker section of the small cave she could not help but ponder the words that had come to her out of the pool in the back of the cave.

There is but one other I can trust? What's the meaning of this?

Sherry was losing hope while at the same time feeling great comfort in knowing that the water born friend was there specifically for her and to give her help and guidance in her captivity. For a brief moment she thought of the note that she had written to Jake and that he was now part of her hope.

Where is he now and what happened to the hackers and terrorists that designed and carried out the attack on Jake's school.

The lack of information and lack of a rescue was beginning to have the effect that the captors wanted. Sherry was gradually unraveling. She was unraveling even though her now nearly constant companion was even more real than ever before.

She turned to the water and said in a voice smitten with frustration, "Ariel, how long must I wait, how many more stones can I remove. How many riddles must I unravel, do you hear me, are you there?"

There was no answer. Just the steady drip, drip, drip of water droplets coming from the small spring in the top of the cave, running their course and eventually leaping off the small stalactite forming in the middle of the cave. Sherry was focused on the smell. The heavy musk was bad enough. Her waste was becoming a problem too. While the liquid she was careful to pour from the collection jars and down the outlet on the far end of the pond. It was however the solid waste that was reviling to her. Her normal routine was to deposit the few pellets she could produce on the pieces of wood then after a drying period she could toss the soiled wood pieces onto the fire. The process worked but she had to shut out the choking odors that she so disliked. She began to long for the days where she took for granted a simple bath in a clean tub. She looked at the black highlights that outlined her fingers.

How ugly I must look. I wasn't made for this I want to be help people, I don't want to waste away in this terrible state.

CHAPTER 21

JANUARY 12, 2001, COLD ICE

The rarely seen shards of sun flooded into the window of the judge's chambers in Seattle. It was a nice day in the middle of a month normally dominated by cold drizzle. At precisely 12:00 PM Judge Blice walked through the door chewing on the final mouth full of the pastrami sandwich he had grabbed on his way back to the office. Both defense and prosecuting attorneys were sitting on opposite corners of the large darkened desk. As he flopped down into the large cordovan leather tufted chair, he heard something about an index of nine.

He turned to the prosecutor, "You, down to a nine now?"

"No Dustin, I was talking about last August. You know I am not going to be golfing, in the rain, in the winter, in Seattle."

"That's right you are worried about getting your hair wet," Blice said with a laugh that started in his mouth and ended in his belly.

"Okay, so what the heck was going on out there the last few minutes?" Judge Blice asked.

"I am just trying to establish that Rollands and Castilano knew each other and that Rollands may have an interest in hiding that fact because it might be embarrassing to a man of his stature in the community; he, being a big time official and all." The defense attorney said.

The prosecutor smiled and looked down at the floor as she said, "You know what you are trying to do is to show that Castilano and Rollands were part of a friendship that went bad and Rollands is just out to get your client."

Blice said, "Okay here is what we are going to do. I will allow your line of questions but if you get out of line, I will shut you down and you can be assured that I will turn into Captain Beligh to you for the rest of the trial, am I clear?"

"I think I got it," the defense attorney chuckled.

"Now for you," Blice said, "where are you headed with this school money stuff Ms. Prosecutor?" He deliberately slowed his speech as he emphasized Ms.

"It is important that the jury understand how much money is at stake here. If Castilano and others would have been successful they could have tapped into not only Cedarvale but Seattle as well. There are some fourteen thousand school districts in the United States and let's say Seattle is average. Then with forty five thousand students and five hundred students per school that's ninety schools. So multiply ninety schools times fourteen thousand school districts that is one million two hundred sixty thousand schools. Let's say Castilano and his group just captured ten dollars per year from each school. That is over twelve million bucks. Not bad for a small terrorist cell" The Prosecutor said.

"Nice argument," Cage said, "but there are many School Districts that only have three or four schools."

"Yes and there are School Districts like New York city with two million students and Los Angeles with over six hundred thousand students." The Prosecutor argued.

KNIGHT JUSTICE

"You have your work cut out for you getting the jury understand this," Blice said.

"Well since the two of you ruined my lunch hour you both owe me, so get outta here and I will see you in a few minutes." Blice laughed.

Moments later, just down the sterile hall the words "all rise" were heard. The large black image of Judge Blice was seen flowing into the court room. The judge found his place behind the large wooden edifice in the front of the courtroom. In the matter of, State v Castilano, State recalls Mr. Ieke Rollands. "You are reminded that you are still under oath," the judge said.

The prosecutor began, "So it is your testimony, Mr. Rollands, that you were jogging along the pier and you saw a raft with Mr. Castilano floating on it. Is that correct?"

The Defense Attorney shot a daggered stare up at the judge but said nothing. Carlos Castilano handed a note with a few scribbles to the defense attorney who wadded the piece up and laid it on the chair next to him.

"Yes,"

"What did you do then?"

"Called the police."

"One last question Mr. Rollands, If someone could tap into the Federal Aid for schools and steal just a few dollars per student. Would that be a lot of money."

"That would be a boat load," Rollands said.

"What is a boat load Sir?"

"Like millions and millions." Rollands said.

The prosecutor said, "That is all I have Your Honor, you are dismissed."

Rollands got up scanned the gallery and walked out of the court slowly. He shot a glance towards two men sitting close to the jury box, as he walked by. Shortly thereafter the two got up and left the court room. They were seen filling Coffee mugs in the hall from the large hot water containers in the conference room next to Judge Blice's court room. A tall person in an all-black outfit walked in and spoke briefly to the men and then left quickly. She was overheard saying something about ice and appeared to drop a large white block into each man's backpack.

"The State calls Cheryl Apostle." The prosecutor said.

Cheryl got up from the bench where she was sitting and walked slowly forward taking her place in the front of the courtroom.

"Please raise your right hand," the bailiff said.

"For the testimony you are about to give do you swear to tell the whole truth and nothing but the truth so help you God?"

"I do," Cheryl breathed.

"Please state your full name and spell it for the record." The prosecutor said.

Small traces of sweat were already starting to appear on Cheryl's forehead.

"Are you Cheryl Apostle?" the prosecutor asked.

"I am," Cheryl replied.

"On the morning of Thursday November 11, 2000, at about 9:40 AM where were you?" The prosecutor asked.

"I was sitting in the office at Cedarvale High School." Cheryl responded.

"Was there anything special about that particular morning?" the prosecutor asked.

"Well yes there was."

"And what was special about the morning of November 11, 2000?" The prosecutor questioned.

KNIGHT JUSTICE

"The first thing is that we had a morning formal assembly. That means it was crazy around there. But what made it totally out of control was that we also had a fire alarm go off during the assembly." Cheryl said.

"Now about what time was that?" the prosecutor queried.

"About 9:42 AM," Cheryl stated.

"Are you sure of the time?" The prosecutor interrupted.

"We have a print out from the fire department," she produced a paper and showed it to the prosecutor as she responded.

"Okay was there anything else special about that day as if that wasn't enough." The prosecutor asked.

Snickers were heard throughout the court. A light tap from the judge's gavel served as a reminder that order must be maintained.

"Well it did create quite a stir, and then I saw that man and another come into the office." Cheryl replied, as she pointed towards Carlos.

"Let the record show that the man she pointed to is Carlos Castilano the defendant.

"Are you sure that is the man you saw?" The prosecutor asked.

"I am," Cheryl replied.

"No further questions at this time your Honor." The prosecutor said.

"Are there questions from the defense?"

"One question your Honor." The defense attorney said.

"You may inquire," the judge allowed.

"You said that the defendant was in your office on November 11, 2000 is that correct?" The defense attorney asked.

"Yes that is correct." Cheryl said.

"Really you are just guessing aren't you?"

"No I am not, it was him."

"How do you know?"

101

"Because, I will never forget those dark piercing eyes and the scar on his right cheek."

No further questions your Honor." The defense attorney said.

The prosecutor requested that the court call Dr. Skecia Thomas. The judge said, "So ordered."

Dr. Thomas made her way to the stand and took her place, just vacated by Cheryl Apostle.

"Raise your right hand. Do you swear to tell the truth and the whole truth so help you God?" the bailiff asked.

"I do," Dr. Thomas said.

"State you full name and spell it for the record. The prosecutor said.

Dr. Thomas replied, "I am Skecia Plit Thomas. Spelled: S k e c i a P l i t T h o m a s."

"Please tell the court what you found the afternoon of November 11, 2000." The Prosecutor said.

"Well, I got a call from Jake Rader and he told me that he had to leave immediately and wanted me to know that he thought some foul play had occurred at Cedarvale. I drove over to the High School Immediately to find the school in a state of disarray."

"When you say disarray what do you mean?" The prosecutor asked.

"Well Fire and Police were at the school, the kids had been sent home and Jake, the principal, was already gone. Cheryl gave me a note stating Jake had left. In essence it said that, one of his teachers had been kidnapped and that the school alarm system had been tampered with. In addition he thought the school business computer might have been tampered with. I called the District Tech. Coordinator who came right over and we discovered that a chip had been added to the computer and that that chip modified the computer so that it would allow access to the district financial system by outside systems.

Police said they had fingerprints from numerous staff as well as the defendant.

"It seems that the defendant had been previously fingerprinted when he was in Washington DC as a member of a Spanish diplomatic family. Upon further investigation it was determined that the defendant was the same person that had told Cheryl that he was a fire department representative."

"No further questions your honor, "the prosecutor said.

The defense attorney got up and walked slowly to the stand.

"Okay so you now are a finger print and computer chip expert, is that what you have testified?" the defense attorney asked.

"No, that is not what I testified. I answered the prosecutor's question as to what I meant by 'things were in disarray'."

"So basically you provided the court with a great deal of unsubstantiated statements we call hearsay in your answer. Is that correct?" The defense attorney asked.

Dr. Thomas said, "Well I shared what I know to be the truth."

Suddenly two men sporting black and white masks rose from their seats and ran to the window, just to the right hand side of the jury box. Then within seconds, the sound of crashing glass filled the room. People started screaming as the sound of small explosions gave rise to an odd and eerie fog escaping from behind the judge.

A guy with a balding head yelled "We're being gassed"

This foreshadowed what was soon to be total chaos. A heavy fog began to fill the room as spectators and jury members alike fled the courtroom. Soon the room was filled with a white mist. Just as the fog reached its peak, three people emerged through a door that led from the judge's quarters. All three were wearing masks. One of them was a woman with a white and black mask covering half of her face. All of a sudden there was a large boom sound then another and finally a third. The sounds were loud but not like explosions.

They were more like percussion that comes from a high pressure differential.

A brief struggle ensued, two officers and a court reporter lay on the floor motionless. Each appeared to have been the loser of a brief scuffle. Barely visible in the heavy mist and fog Carlos Castilano was seen joining the three intruders as people dove through a window that had been broken out by small percussive blasts.

A total of four divers left through the partially opened windows. Each diver landed in the large dump truck. The truck bed was filled with a large air filled mattress. The landing pad according to one witness had the words "Seattle Public Schools" written on one end. Another saw what seemed to be a big pillow in the back of a huge truck. Carlos and the others were now resting on a gradually deflating cushion. The air in the mattress slowly escaped leaving the four escapees hidden in the back of the truck. The truck made a right turn and continued west towards the waterfront. There was a great deal of confusion surrounding the events. No clear story emerged, yet a reporter from a local paper was a witness. This is the story told by the reporter. That witness had been sitting in on the trial reporting on the proceeding for the Renton Valley News.

The truck continued straight down towards the waterfront. Not more than ten minutes after it all started it was over. Moments later the four jumped out of the rig. It was stopped at a light. As it sat there the dump bed gradually started to rise. As the bed rose, the large steel paneled gate on the back of the truck opened to about eighteen inches. The four rolled out under the truck's gate and walked right out onto the pier.

Two minutes later the four stepped onto a 50 foot yacht. The skipper cast off the lines and the large Cummins engines rumbled as the boat slowly made its way out of the harbor and headed across Elliott Bay toward the Straits. Meanwhile throngs of officers and police were seen streaming into the superior court building. There was no evidence of damage except for a burst steam pipe and one window that seemed to have been blown open. No residue or any foreign object was located. Two Seattle officers and a bailiff were in the courtroom seemingly sleeping. When questioned later they gave conflicting and confusing stories of the events.

CHAPTER 22

Jan 14, 2001, The Order

Since I had spent the better part of two days in the caves and tunnels I needed to get out for a while. Rather than crawl through the back end of the underground castle where I started, I was guided to the old abandoned ranch house that sat on the grounds of an old mine. It was a long walk out of the massive hall that accessed the basement of the old house. I opened a large metal door that was on the far end of an old coal storage bin. I walked through the basement and up the stairs. Finally I walked out the front door. The house sat atop of a large mountain. Looking from the house there was no obvious evidence of the huge castle cave sitting below the mountain top. I spent the morning and early afternoon, sitting in the woods, alone, contemplating what I had heard and seen. The beauty and majesty of creation was overwhelming me.

As I watched two doe and a buck frolic below, I was thankful and happy, yet I could not stop thinking of my kids at home and Sherry. As was my usual practice I slowly relaxed and focused on the beauty of creation. I felt myself slowly transform into an eagle. I was soaring above the cliffs looking down on the earth below. It was beautiful.

Around 3:00 PM I left the woods, walked back to my room and quickly ate the soup and toast that awaited my return. As I finished my last bite of bread, three figures dressed in black with a white cross outlined in red on their chest approached me and bound my hands behind my back and led me across the hall. They tied me to a chair. A black hood was placed over my head.

I was seated on a simple wooden chair, my feet were tied to the legs of the chair and there I sat. It seemed to be hours, yet most likely, it was much less than that. After the long period of silence I began to hear what sounded to me like one of the old "Mystery of the Air," programs on the radio that I used to listen to when I was a kid. You know, the announcer with the baritone voice reading a script while ominous music rose and fell in the background.

For what must have been at least an hour, I heard the voice reciting basic factual information.

The voice said, "The Hospitallers were originally monks dedicated to provide for and help the sick and the poor. The Knights of St. John know the code of Chivalry and TRICHS. The battle is for hearts and minds not prestige and pride. Honor is given only, none takes Honor."

On and on the recitations unfolded as I sat in my voluntary captivity and humility. On and on the music droned. I was simply trapped in a bad dream of my own choosing. I knew that if I wanted to I could have freed myself from the boring and yet intriguing drone. But the longer that I sat there the more I was seduced by the nature of what I was about to do. I was on the beginning of a life transformation. I was moving from the day to day struggles of mundane into the quest for extraordinary significance. What a few short weeks earlier would have been to me the goofiest and most ridiculous event, was now becoming significant and amazing. What I would have run from I was now embracing. I began to smile to myself as the hours passed.

I was beginning to see what those young Nobles most likely saw so many centuries earlier. I could be part of a brotherhood not of men. I was becoming part of a brotherhood of giving. I began to sob, and then I began to laugh out loud. I would drift into a kind of sleep or trance then back to my reality. I was a captive of my mind and my trust. I was a time traveler back a thousand years and forward to present and then back again. On each trip back I learned, on my trip forward, I refined my learning. Then it was over.

Just as I was so abruptly brought into my captivity, I was so released. First my feet then my hands and with a swish my dark hood was gone and there I was, seated in nothing but shorts and socks. I was in a dark room only partially lit by candles. I saw what seemed to me to be hundreds of red robed men each with a Maltese cross held to their chest and each looking at me. It was at that moment that I noticed the music was gone and there was an eerie silence. I just looked straight ahead. I noticed that Chris was now standing directly before me. He lit the large candle that set atop a cross. He set it on the small table before me. I thought to myself, *is this real, am I in my skivvies in front of these guys and only a bit self-conscious?*

Chris said, "Arise and take your candle."

I slowly and a bit clumsily took the candle.

"What will you do with your candle?"

I looked around the room at the dimly lit faces and thought. *Now is the time to be very clear.* I answered, "I want to give it back to the brotherhood to let it shine for the poor and the sick."

Suddenly the candle was snatched from my hands, doused and I was grabbed and ushered from the room. I was literally tossed into my room. Before I was able to catch wind of what just happened I was face to face with Christian and the old Native American.

"Why would you say such a thing?" Christian asked, "You being the son of a minister and all." You give it to God. That is the whole point of your training," Christian said.

I was humiliated and distraught, I said, "You should have prepared me, you are my mentors."

A tear formed in the corner of the Old Man's eye as he bit his lower lip.

"You know what this means?" he asked.

"I am out of the Knights?" I asked.

Christian said, "Get dressed; we will see you next door in five minutes."

As the door closed I was alone and bewildered. I looked around the room as I pulled on my shirt and wranglers. I now realized how much I would miss the people I had become close to. It now was clear that to serve in this order would have been what I wanted. I vowed right then and there that I would not stop until I was a Knight, If not with these guys, a Knight on my own. *Sherry is out there and there are so many that can use my help.*

I looked at my watch and saw the time. It was 6:00AM, I had been in this nightmare all night long. I put on my remaining clothes, tied my red and white tennis shoe laces. I took my papers and books in my small pack. I left it on the desk and slowly walked out of the room. I made my way across the hall and opened the door to the great room. I started in. Then I heard a roar and celebration.

"Congratulations," the Old Man yelled.

What? I thought to myself.

The room was bright. All the lights were on. I was about to be welcomed into the brotherhood. I had not made a mistake. As I learned later, I had already passed all the tests. I was already accepted, I was a member. I had successfully endured months of training and weeks of deprivation, this qualified me. The celebration was to be a confirmation that I was about to be welcomed as a member. Now I had to think about the huge responsibility I was to take on as a Knight of St. John. Atop the large table that, just moments before separated me from the others in the room was now bidding me a warm welcome. Breakfast was prepared and a party was taking place in my honor. You see the way you give to God is by giving to others is what I learned.

I sobbed.

CHAPTER 23

JANUARY 15, 2001, BACKGROUND INFORMATION

Christian Poincy, the Delta Sigma Knight sat in front of his council. The council consisted of seven Sigma Knights. He was the sixth Delta Sigma since De'Berry who had been appointed and confirmed in his clandestine role by Paul the first, the only protestant Grand Master in the history of the order. Christian had been elevated to his position a decade earlier and had run the military arm in secret and according to the code.

He started by reviewing the status. "I have been told that if in fact the chip that was planted in the computer at Ceadervale would have been activated the damage would have been great. There would have been possibly billions disappear from the National Treasury. It seems that there are limited security measures in place when the attack comes from the inside and that is exactly what we had. You all know that there are only a very few people in our ranks that understand this stuff. One of them happens to be Sherry Paul and she is out of commission at the moment. We need her to help us figure out how this group is gaining access to the computer systems. I think you are all aware of the problem we face. Not only did they get to the school computer they also controlled the government computers of the city. We need Sherry to help figure this out.

I have just received word from Scotland Yard and confirmed with sources in the United States security agencies, that we likely have a traitor in our order. While the evidence is strong in my opinion, careful and thoughtful action will be required if we expect to expose the traitor and to save Sherry Paul. While we cannot be totally sure, we are confident, that Sherry is okay. They know her value. Yet prudence dictates that we cannot wait much longer to act. I have good information that the recent and dramatic jail break involving Carlos Castilano, as well as the capture and hiding of Sherry was in fact the brain child of one of our own. The good news is that we now have good evidence as to the where Sherry is and even how she is doing."

Alberto the dark haired and sturdily built Spaniard asked, "How does this impact our plans for Jake Rader and any role he might have in a rescue attempt?"

"Our hunches were correct." Christain replied. "We are now, quite sure that she is being held in one of our caves within the matrix, somewhere here in New Mexico. Therefore we will need a full assessment of all potential sites and a rescue plan. Jake will, I am sure, contribute well during the process. Let's make sure however, that Jake does not end up like Sherry or worse. He is a good one."

Alberto said, "I am sure that can be worked out."

"What are the details as we now know them?" Antonio asked.

"It is likely that Sherry has been hidden in a cave within our cavelet system, the FBI has been following a fellow by the name of Kareem Razier. He was located in Durango Colorado at some dive apartment, he's been there for a while now." Christian observed.

Antonio interrupted, "Wait a minute I don't understand why we haven't just searched the cavelet system and found Sherry."

"Let me answer this one," the old Native American said. "First off," he continued, "there are literally thousands if not tens of thousands of underground facilities in the desert southwest and Colorado. We have no idea where to begin. Some of these caves are connected to the nuke siloes, some are covered with rocks like at Mesa Verde and others are still inside high security areas like area 51 and Roswell. You can't just walk in and look around most of these areas."

"All right I understand we don't want to draw a lot of attention at this point," Antonia said, "but we must have some idea, right?"

"As I was saying," the Old Man said, "The CIA tapped Kareem Razier's phone. That is how he was located in Durango. We are now fairly convinced that she is in the Mesa Verde area. In fact we believe her to be somewhere off Wetherill Mesa. The reason is that as we have been told the mustangs roaming that area seem to be hanging out in one draw that has a number of cavelets. A ranger said she thought she saw smoke coming from the back side of the draw the other day and there are no campgrounds or campsites allowed in that area. We have authorization to do surveillance on that area starting tomorrow at 6:00 AM.

In a recent conversation, Razier was given orders to 'finish her off '. These orders came from a cell phone that had been purchased in Seattle, Washington and the voice of the person giving the orders may be our 'mastermind'. Quantico is in the process of doing a voice study. As such you are to be very careful in this rescue attempt.

We are getting the best voice analysis we can. Frankly that is the main reason we have not moved in already. The unfortunate fact is, that if this is one of our own we need to make sure we snare him at the same time we safely extricate Sherry. We think she may well be in poor condition. That is why time is now of the essence. Are there further questions and or comments? If not, Alberto don't screw this up."

"We won't Sir," Antonio responded.

CHAPTER 24

JANUARY 18, 2001, RENEGADE REUNION

Kareem Razier stepped into the rented cargo van and drove twenty-two hours straight through to a small harbor just south of Sausalito, California.

I am really good he thought as he drove right to the pier he had been told to bring the auto to.

He was waiting at the slip as the fifty foot cruiser glided into the pilings. Carlos Castilano and two others jumped to shore on the dock from the fantail.

"Long time no see, ya SOB." Carlos yelled as he grabbed Razier in a bearhug.

"It's about time you showed up, I was about to declare you lost at sea." Razier replied.

Carlos winced as Kareem grabbed his hand.

"Careful, I think I broke my hand when I dove out of the courtroom." Carlos said.

"Dove out of a court room; what do you mean?" Razier asked.

"You didn't hear," Carlos said, "We jumped out of the court room into a school dump truck."

He smirked as he thought of the smucks that were left dazed on the courtroom floor as he and the others disappeared through the blown out court house windows. "The only problem is that I hit my hand on the side wall of the truck as I was landing. Forty feet is a long drop out of a window. It was pretty exciting. What a rush, I wish I could have seen the old SOB judge's face when we all escaped out of the window. He must have had apoplexy or at least a stroke." Carlos declared.

"Where is the big guy?" Razier asked as they headed toward the van.

"He will meet us in Durango after we pick up our chick." Carlos said sarcastically.

"Are you guy's hungry?" Razier asked as he turned the rig to the north.

One of the guys in the back said, "Starving."

Razier said, "There is a Carl's Jr. 20 minutes down the I-101."

"Sounds good to me," Carlos said while peering over the top of the girly magazine he was scanning.

"Okay, so what do we do with Sissy when we get her?" Razier asked.

Sissy is the name that Carlos coined for Sherry Paul while making fun of her. That was early the year before when Carlos and Razier were originally recruited to kidnap Sherry and to help steal money from the United States Department of Education. They were warned by the big guy that she was a very capable person well acquainted with self-defense techniques. To Carlos a woman could never be a physical threat. He never really saw any threat at all.

"We take her to Durango and give her to the big guy and he gives us our $500,000 each." Carlos declared.

"How can we be sure he will pay up?" Razier asked.

"Because if he doesn't, I go back to Seattle and turn myself in and agree to testify against him. At least that is what he thinks I will do." Carlos said.

As the van pulled into the parking lot Razier's phone rang. The others headed into the Carls Jr. burger joint while Razier stayed in the vehicle talking on the phone.

"Yeah, I got em." Razier answered.

The voice on the other end of the phone said, "When do you think you slackers will be back here?"

"We should be there by the weekend." Razier said.

"Okay see you then." The phone went silent.

Razier pushed the red button on his cell phone, slid out of the front seat, and headed in to get a burger. In less than 20 minutes the four were back on the road headed towards Oakland on the I-80. Later that evening the group pulled into a small dusty, wind-blown, one story motel made of cinder block. The peeling white paint gave the appearance of grey and white texture. It looked like the coat of an Appaloosa pony. It was just off the intersection of I-40 and highway 97 outside Kingman, Arizona.

Carlos looked at the large silver and turquoise ring he had purchased just months earlier. For just a moment he wondered how many poor slobs had risked life and limb in the process of mining the silver and precious metals so that he could show it off.

Isn't it interesting, he thought, *I am wearing the tailing of a mine just a few miles from here on my finger?* He laughed out loud as the transport in which they were traveling pulled to a stop in the dingy motel parking lot.

CHAPTER 25

JANUARY 18, 2001, SALT LIGHT

Looking down at a dust covered finger, Sherry noticed how black and broken her fingernails were. She had just finished her fourth round of 25 pushups and 50 sit-ups. She was beginning to find an ironic power in that, while she was weakened and still struggling with her confined and squalid state; she had now accepted her plight. From time to time she noticed that she was quite dizzy and suffered headaches often. She didn't really dwell on the problems because she knew that she was not the picture of excellent health. She was well aware of those that had endured extreme hardship. She knew that survivors were those who maintained a positive outlook.

She wasn't discouraged in that as of yet, she could not move the large boulders that were blocking her escape. Her attempts to use the logs and poles found within the cave were futile but they gave her incentive to try. By now nearly all of the poles were cracked, broken or burned for warmth. She eyed the pickets she had placed above the opening to her large underground cell. She wondered if she had made a mistake in using these valuable assets for spears to protect against her capturers at the moment of truth.

Can I really repel an attack with such a simple weapon made of small, painstakingly stone sharpened logs?

Each log was lashed to the next by the threads she had carefully unraveled from the bottom of what had been beautiful jeans. The log pickets were hung at the entrance just below a rough wooden shelf she had built of log fragments and stones. The stones she had been able to extract from the cave opening. The plan was to grab the pickets and slash them against any would-be-attacker, she could make a last ditch escape attempt at just the right moment. Sherry knew her chances of success were limited; as she figured Razier and Boyd would send at least three to get her. She was at peace with the fact that they might never come back to get her. In this case she might well end up as the dust and stone fragments of the cave herself. She knew that she was down to her last few weeks of nuts to eat.

"Ariel, please hear me," Sherry said.

Soon there was the familiar sound of water rushing through the cave and the image Sherry had become comfortable watching and communicating with, that was now in full view just above the surface of the water.

Sherry spoke first, "I now know what you want of me."

Then the visage slowly said, "And of what have you been thinking?

"I have deeply thought about the key to life," Sherry said.

"And what is the key?" Ariel quized.

"When I help I grow," Sherry said.

"How so?" Ariel asked.

"I now see it like this; I respond to and invest in the best interest of others then I gain their trust and respect. As such I earn the right to influence their thoughts, responses and investments. I gain while I provide a service in the way we as Knights are supposed to." Sherry said.

KNIGHT JUSTICE

"And what have you determined about your enemies?" Ariel asked.

"The same is true for enemies. The enemy wants to use me for their purposes. To the extent that I can help them, I use the opportunity to earn their respect. There is a problem. When my enemy is hurting my friend. At that point I must repel the enemy of my friend. If of course the friend is doing right. It is a matter of degree. If I cause great harm even to an enemy then I am of little good. I need to insure that the greatest good is done for all. You know the old adage, "first do no harm," to the best of my ability. If I can do this without causing harm, then all grow." Sherry added confidently.

"You are growing in the Knight," Ariel asserted, "You will shortly have a chance to invest in your growth."

"What do you mean?" Sherry asked as the image slowly faded back into the depths of the pool. *Does this mean it's almost over?*

CHAPTER 26

JANUARY 19, 2001, STRIKE FORCE

I felt the stone's texture as I fingered the Clovis point. It was by now my most cherished possession. I stared down at the Maltese cross that was inlayed onto the Clovis point that had made its way full circle. I thought fondly of the story of its journey so many years earlier. It had come from the river valley possibly in south Texas. Then it was carried with the Native Americans who guided new friends, the small group of Knights as they reestablished their military order in the "New World". The ancient spear-point was then traded to the plains Indians and eventually given to my grandfather.

It had been entrusted to me and I had squandered that trust by giving it to Sherry so many years earlier. As the mysteries of life so often dictate, she returned it to me as an act of love, strangely now; I was very likely in a position to get it back to Sherry. At least that is what I hoped.

I smiled as I thought about the Maltese people who had learned their truth from a man named Paul who took refuge from a storm in a cave on an island. That very same island provided safety to the

Knights of Saint John who shared with and learned from the Maltese people the truths of Paul the Apostle. The very same principles I now regard as part of my personal Philosophy. I was committed at this moment and from each and every tick of the clock to uphold. I was beginning my first mission as a warrior. I was ready to use what I had learned not only the skills developed in my youth, but also the learnings of the past few months. We were on the war path as we planned to rescue a gal by the name of Sherry Paul.

Strange how life turns round and round as we roll along.

As I sat and pondered all that had transpired during the past year, I began to wonder.

Is it possible, that I had really begun what was a crazy, foolish chase after Sherry and the strange new life she has shared with me? Is there a Nightingale effect for guys?

The answer to these and the thousands of questions still swirling through my soul had to wait. For at that very moment the reality of my new life was knocking at my door. I grasped the leather straps that held the stone point as I stood up.

Antonio and four others walked into the room as I attached the Clovis point onto my neck via the leather straps.

"Are you ready," Antonio yelled.

"Sure am sir," I yelled back.

"Let's go get her then," he directed with a smile.

I grabbed my small backpack and followed Antonio and the others out into the great hall which led to a portal that led up a long pristine underground tunnel. The tunnel led to a small seating area in the middle of what looked like an underground train station. It wasn't large, possibly only a few meters across. Down below I saw what looked like a single rail or steel beam that ran along the concrete floor. We walked through the station. On the far side were stairs. We walked up the wood slatted stairs. As we arrived at the top of the stairs I heard a whooshing sound and noticed a white capsule fill the space just to our left.

With the sound of air pressure releasing a large oval door popped open. We walked inside what appeared to be a transport of some form. As the cat walked in behind us, the large door swung shut. It finally locked into place after moving in slowly against the black rubber insulation.

A unisex monotone voice said, "Please take a seat we are leaving in ten, nine, eight … seconds." I sat down just as I began to feel the acceleration. I noticed that there were a few round portals on the curved walls of the vehicle. I was seated next to one.

CHAPTER 27

AT THE SAME TIME, RAT PACK

At a spot not more than 50 miles away another group was forming. While they did not know it, this band was getting ready to counter the efforts of the Knights. They thought they were going to continue to enslave Sherry while they managed to extract the last bit of life from her own control.

"Great to see you," Carlos coughed over the large cigar hanging from his lips as he caught sight of the figure immerging from behind a large rock on the top of the hill.

"It's about time you showed up," was the reply.

It was late in day and the sun's rays were carving clear straight lines through the distant gauze like clouds.

"We don't have a lot of time, so let's get a move on," Carlos said to the others.

"Hold your horses," the group leader said, "I want you to bring her back to me once you retrieve her from her cozy cottage. You understand, I want her in good shape. Boyd do you hear me?"

Boyd said nothing.

"We will have her back to this very spot in less than an hour." Carlos replied.

Five people were standing in a draw not more than one hundred yards from a vacant spot in Mesa Verde National park. Razier shot a reflexive glance over his back as if he was expecting someone else to show up.

Carlos noticed and queried sarcastically, "What's wrong, are you nervous, kitty master?"

While Razier did not reply, the glare he shot in the direction of Carlos was clear enough. The tension in the air was heavy as the four made their way through the pinion pine and dense underbrush that filled the natural cut in the earth. Four men walked and sometimes crawled, slowly deeper into the draw. No one in the group knew that Carlos Castilano was packing a small wafer of silicone and silver under his skin. It was a small tracking devise.

⋏

While Carlos was sleeping in his bunk months earlier a guard made his way into the cell. He grabbed Carlos by the arms, picked him up and slammed him against the wall.

"You had better tell us where Sherry Paul is, you dirty piece of camel dung," the guard said.

Carlos laughed as he spit in the guards face. The guard walked out of the cell and locked the door behind. Carlos grabbed under his arm as he felt a sharp pain like he had been scratched or pinched in the pit. What he did not know was that the guard had plunged the small devise just under his skin. Carlos walked back over to his bunk and laid down. He even felt the welt towards the edge of his latissimus dorsi muscle, as he began to calm back down. Soon he was sleeping again.

That was the last he thought of the incident. Yet, the small transmitter allowed those who knew the frequency to track and to receive transmissions for the next year to within just a few yards. He was a small dot on the computer screen sitting on the lap of Antonio the Beta Knight. Antonio, Christian, myself and two others were levitating through tunnels under New Mexico at breakneck speed, in the direction of Mesa Verde.

CHAPTER 28

JANUARY 19, 2001, CAVE CHAOS

Nearly 25 horses gathered outside the small flattened area on a large ledge that I guessed, served as Sherry Paul's prison for forty days. At least that is what I thought I was seeing through my field glasses. The daily treat of oats and barley was just what the mustangs and domesticated horses craved now. Every evening, without fail, just as the sun was fading and the shadows of the canyon grew large throughout the valley, a Cessna 172 dropped pound bags of oats from 500 feet above the valley floor. The bags crashed to the ground in just that spot. Inside Sherry could hear and feel the rumble of their arrival that day as had been the routine each and every day the past six weeks. Early in her confinement Sherry would unleash cries for help to no avail. As her hope of rescue dimmed so did this ritual.

After well over a month of depravation, Sherry barely took note other than to realize that another day was winding down. Today however something was different. She heard activity on the other side of the opening. She began to hear the sound of *human* activity.

The stones are being removed.

Suddenly a flush of excitement began to flow through her veins.

Instinctively she began to yell, "Help are you out there can you hear me?" "Help, help me!" There was no response. As she listened more closely she could hear the sound of scraping and rumbling like thunder and ocean waves crashing on the beach all mingled together. She realized that the sounds were generated by huge boulders scratching across the earth. Outside the cave, two domestic horses roped to the huge boulders were being driven by one of the men along with Carlos and Razier.

CHAPTER 29

AN HOUR EARLIER,
HERO'S WELCOME

As we were about to be deposited in Mesa Verde park, Antonio looked back at me and said, "Hey buddy, how are you doing, you look like you are going to a funeral, all dark and sullen."

"Just getting my game face on," I responded in a feeble attempt to convince everyone in the capsule that I was up to the challenge.

Deep inside it was a very different story. I had been going through all the various scenarios I could imagine. Not one of the images included dealing with teams of horses dragging boulders.

I thought about all the possible greetings that Carlos and Kareem and the unknown others might have for us. What weapons would they have with them? I ruled out most large and or technologically advanced weapons. These guys, at the end of the day, were working with limited funds. They were in fact, two-bit terrorists. I thought they might have handguns, possibly small Luger style. They very likely had stolen thirty-eight caliber or nine mm pistols. These would be small and fairly easy to conceal, especially in California. I thought they had come through California

KNIGHT JUSTICE

and did not want to risk a search by California authorities, who took gun control very seriously.

I had convinced myself that if we were careful, our element of surprise would work well. If the surprise worked, we would not need fire power. Remember we were in a national park. A gun battle would not be in their best interest and certainly not in ours. All anyone would need were the sounds of gun shots ringing out across the canyons. Yet, what if Antonio and Chris had been wrong, what if these cowards had a lot of people rather than the three or four that we expected? What if they had scanners or other devises that we did not anticipate? I looked back at the young cougar lying on the carpet next to the door.

The young cat was sleeping as he did most of the time. Gil was our best and most unique asset. The young, still a bit wild cougar, loved to chase anything that moved. I had experienced that myself.

How did Chris train the cat to chase people rather than rabbits and or other living things we might see out in the dry cliff country?

I had learned in my recent training that I could worry without letting the worry turn to fear. Now unlike a few months earlier I was able to plan and put my trust in the competence of others; this included Gil. Just the same, I needed to review all the plans. I was disappointed that the others in the capsule could read me so easily.

The capsule was equipped with large monitors that continuously showed images of the surrounding countryside. These monitors somehow wirelessly provided visual details of the area, much like a split screen TV screen. I noticed that the pictures seemed to be in real time and that the detail of the environment above ground was captured in excellent contrast. We literally were able to see a 360 degree picture of the outside while zooming along underground. I assumed there must have been some satellite feed that somehow tracked our progress and relayed images in real time. The vehicle was smooth and quiet. I noticed that we were weaving our way back and forth across the numerous switchbacks that lead up the canyons back to the area not too far from Wetherill mesa.

"How do you like the ride?" Antonio asked with a smile.

"I feel like I am on Mercury, if you want to know the truth." I replied.

As we zipped past one section I made out what I thought was the last camping area I had been briefed on. There I caught a glimpse of what I thought to be Ieke Rollands. He was sitting in a van just outside a park turnaround. It was just past the last camping area in the most isolated area of the park.

I should mention it to Chris and the others. Then again they might think my notice a bit odd. I had not seen him in months. There was no indication he might be in Mesa Verde. *What would he be doing in this area anyway?*

As the capsule continued on toward the end of the tunnel, I thought back on my own grand-dad. In my stream of consciousness I saw myself sitting on his lap and he was shaking the last few small round pellets of his sugar substitute into the cream and coffee filled cup. Every once and a while I would get a sniff of Hills Brothers coffee and think I saw him. It is not like I really believed he was there. It is more like I wanted the comfort that he provided me when I was very young. At the age of four or five the smell and the taste of fresh brewed coffee and graham crackers imprinted on my brain. He would dip the graham crackers into the coffee and give me a taste. I loved those times when I knew that everything I needed, my grandfather would provide while I was safe on his lap. In the same way I was now confusing the times I had with Sherry at the lake and the fact that I first met Ieke Rollands during that same trip.

While Ieke was strong and confident he was now a constant negative image in my head. Those times I shared with Sherry just a few months earlier stirred emotions from what was now a distant and never to be seen again childhood and the island and my grandfather and Sherry were linked. But Ieke Rollands was there as an image of what I hated.

My mental meanderings were brought back to reality when all of a sudden Chris yelled; "get out," to Antonio. "They are here, not more than a mile below us," he exclaimed.

I looked back through a portal as a cloud of vapor began to descend on the now rapidly decelerating capsule.

Gil suddenly raised his head and let out a sound like a grunt if to say, "Let's get to it."

Yet with all my planning and the preparations made by my new colleagues, how could we know they were to use horses. How would Gil, a natural born predator react to a natural prey?

Meanwhile not more than a mile away mustangs and men were preparing the final phases of the "Sherry trap". It was designed to inflict mental and physical pain on what was now a changed woman. Little did the hostage handlers know that a new and steeled Sherry Paul would soon be emerging from her 40 days of solitary confinement stronger than ever.

CHAPTER 30

JANUARY 16, 2001, CAT CAGE

It was nearly dark as the harness clad mustangs pulled the last of the huge boulders from the mouth of the cave. It had been much easier to slide and roll the boulders down the tunnel of the cave prison. A few men accomplished this in less than an hour. Now horses were needed to do the trick. The nets that were used to drag the boulders from their perch were the very same nets that were designed to snare Sherry as she experienced freedom for a brief moment.

Carlos yelled to Kareem across the draw, "If the net doesn't snare her, stampede the mustangs and the other net tied to your ponies should get her. As a last resort shoot her."

Kareem Razier nodded in agreement. He fingered the handle of the nine mm Ruger hanging at his side. He was beginning to wonder why he was in the position he was in. Somehow preparing to drag a woman through the thickets and brambles of the desert of western New Mexico were beginning to wear on him.

Why am I here? He thought as the mustangs snorted and stirred inches from his rocky perch. It was as if the wild horses could sense the injustice of it all, a young woman trapped in a cage was about to be drug and humiliated for the mere pleasure of a few sick and deranged souls. Carlos was the sickest of them all. At least he was the only one Kareem had ever mentioned with a total lack of respect. I overheard Razier say something about that slimy Carlos just before the attack at Cedarvale months earlier. At that moment, Razier was reflecting on the man back in the van the big boss, *now that is real slime.*

CHAPTER 31

THE SAME TIME, CAGED LION

Inside the cave, Sherry was frantically moving the last of the smaller rocks from the cave entrance. Tied to her tattered blouse were three large sticks each about eight inches long. Each was sharpened to a point. They had been her last project while confined to the cave. She had honed the points by rubbing the end repeatedly against the sandstone wall of the cave. The result was a nice collection of wooden daggers. The sticks banged against her waist as she carefully made her way out towards the cave entrance.

CHAPTER 32

THE SAME TIME, KNIGHT RESPONSE

and the others were just coming over the hill. We had carefully and slowly picked our way down the cliffs and crags as much with the fading sunlight at our backs was possible.

"It looks like there are four of them. Is that what you see Jake?" Antonio whispered to me.

"Is that Carlos on that boulder just over the rise?" I said.

"Yes and you see the two at the bottom just outside the mouth of the cave?" Antonio whispered.

"I do. What are all the horses down there doing?"

Antonio dropped his night vision goggles from his eyes, "it looks like they have been dragging boulders from the opening of the cave."

"See the two in the middle," I said. "I think they are dragging a net of some kind."

"Yeah I see it." He breathed.

I whispered back, "I just picked up Razier; he is on a large boulder about fifty yards southwest of the cave entrance. See, right in the middle of the horses grazing in that open patch?"

135

"I see him." Antonio said.

At a location nearly 100 yards away Chris and the Old Man were focused on the horses too. Unfortunately they couldn't see the net that we saw.

"Okay," the old Native American said, "It's about dark and the horses are restless. Something is about to happen and they can sense it."

Chris and Gil just sat on a large boulder.

"I am going to send Gil down through the bottom; that should scatter the horses."

"Jake you take Razier and we will get Carlos and the others, will not be easy." Antonio said.

"I just hope that lion remembers she is to chase down a human and not those big four legged beasts," Chris said, as he sent Gil down the draw.

Inside the entrance of the cave a wild scene was developing. Through my glasses I saw a guy with a tattoo of an x and a crescent moon on his arm, slowly make his way into the cave entrance. What I could not see was happening next. I did however see the result and it was not pretty. Suddenly the guy emerged from the entrance of the cave. He staggered to the path and fell to his knees. As I looked closer I noticed what appeared to be a small section of a picket fence sticking through his chest. Right below the abdomen a small log with a pointed tip protruded and as he fell to his knees, blood flowed, and he was writhing there on the ground. At that very moment Sherry emerged from the cave opening, she took a few steps forward and everything came unglued.

Through my glasses I saw that she began to run and at the same time the two mustangs still attached to the net bolted. The little cat started off on a tear, in the direction of the horses and Sherry.

I felt a shot of adrenalin as I took off in the direction of Razier. I moved low to the ground so that I would not be seen by those in the valley below. I shot a glance back as I saw Antonio head out in the direction of Carlos. Moving as fast as I could I was able to see a large net jet from above the opening of the cave and ensnare Sherry. She hit the ground hard as the horses continued at a gallop up the path toward a sheer rock cliff. I was now moving as fast as possible as I saw the cat go airborne. The small cat then turned her attention on human prey. Seconds later, Gil hit Razier with the force of a small locomotive and knocked him head over heels in my direction. Now at a full run I pounced on Razier driving my head straight into his abdomen. He was on his back on the ground gasping for air. I grabbed his hands.

The young cat was now on the heels of about five or six horse's driving them back into the direction of Carlos. As I finished wrapping tape around Razier's hands and feet I heard Carlos screaming in the background.

"Don't let him eat me," he yelled, "don't let him eat me." I could hear the blood-curdling sound of the cat growling in the background.

The whole incident lasted less than five minutes and it was over. Carlos and Razier were subdued and I was standing on the path with my foot on Razier's neck. I raised my new dust covered night goggles to my eyes. I could see Sherry still caught in the net being pulled slowly up the path ahead. I pushed down vigorously on Razier's neck and he choked.

I yelled to Chris who was 10 yards away. "I am going after Sherry."

I started up the hill at a brisk jog. As I moved along the trail I noticed bits of clothing and an occasional drop of blood. I could see that there was damage to the shrubs and bushes as the net had been dragged along the ground with Sherry trapped inside. About a minute later I crested the hill and saw that the snare had been torn loose of the horses and they stood chewing on grass a mere 100 yards ahead.

I looked over the edge of the steep ravine with my goggles and could make out what I thought might be Sherry about 100 feet below my location.

I yelled down with my hands cupped over my mouth, "Sherry, are you down there?"

There was no response.

Again I yelled, "Sherry, are you okay?"

No response!

I started to pick my way down the ledge to what seemed to be an outcropping just above what I thought to be her position. As I slid down the rocky pitch half on my feet and half on my rear I landed on the ledge. I heard my body thump as I slammed onto the rocky ledge. I felt a sharp stinging sensation on the back of my head. Slightly dazed, I stood up. In my head mounted flashlight I could see I was face to face with none other than Ieke Rollands. He was smiling. He smiled with that same smile I had seen when he was sitting at his big desk in downtown Seattle a few months earlier.

"Hey sport how ya doing?" He asked in that pride filled way I had remembered and reacted negatively to at the time.

I just stared at him. I knew he was up to no good and I was the man to stop him. I did not flinch.

"Glad you are here, now help me get down and help Sherry," he ordered.

As he spoke, I noticed him reaching inside his military jacket. Out of instinct, luck or divine province, I moved in on him and grabbed him pinning his arms above mine. He struck back hard with his knee. I was prepared. I wheeled around as I used his momentum against him. While I felt his knee make contact with my mid-thigh it made no major impact. Force allowed me to pivot and roll him across my body. He was now propelled toward the rock wall. As we both slammed into a large boulder he was under me. I felt his back crack as he slumped backwards over the rock. His head banged hard against the ledge wall as did mine. He was still working to get inside his coat when I heard a voice behind me. I finally pinned my elbows against the ground while pushing Rolland's Adam's apple nearly through the back of his throat with my head.

"What is going on here," Christian yelled as he descended to our position. The lion was nearly on his heels.

"I have cornered this rat and he is the one behind this whole thing," I yelled as I continued to press hard against his throat. "Look here, he tried to shoot me."

Chris pulled Rolland's coat back and there under Rolland's jacket was a Ruger nine mm fully loaded and ready to do damage.

Chris grabbed the gun and pointed it at Ieke's forehead.

"Now Chris," Rollands said. "You and I go back a very long way. Flaky Jake here is wacky."

"Get up we will sort this out later," Chris said.

"Jake now get down there and help Sherry."

Dizzy and disoriented, I picked up the head light off the ground and replaced it on my cap. I was a bit dazed and confused; yet, I was still feeling a rush of emotions as I headed down the steep pitch to the motionless Sherry just 20 feet below. I glanced back to see Chris and Ieke Rollands heading back up the trail. Gil walked slowly behind with her tail moving in a slow metronomic rhythm. I knew that Chris must not have wanted Rollands anywhere near Sherry at that moment.

CHAPTER 33

January 19, 2001, Life Death

I carefully slid down the last few yards that separated me from Sherry. As I bounced and scrambled down the rocky outcroppings I could see her bruised and broken body lying in a heap. She was not moving. As I crawled closer, I noticed blood on the ground; not a good sign. I leaned over her and placed my ear on her face. It was cool but not cold. I could not hear her breathing.

"Sherry," I whispered, "Sherry can you hear me. It's Jake."

No response...

As I knelt down beside her I looked at her dirty, torn and tattered clothes. Her right arm which was closest to me was badly injured. I carefully picked up her arm and felt her wrist for a pulse. I could not detect one.

I then thought I heard her whisper something like, "Shinea or See kinda or something like that."

I said, "Sherry you are alright, I know you'll be fine." She whispered in a slow and halting way, "Follow Ariel Aion."

That made no sense to me. As she completed the last sound I became more concerned. I did not want to risk moving her because from the looks of it, she may have had any number of internal or back injuries.

I yelled out, "Oh my God, please help us, somebody." Just as I was completing my cries for help, Gil strode up and sat at my side. In the darkness I could see that Gil had in her mouth the Clovis point necklace I had lost in my struggle with Ieke Rollands. I instinctively grabbed the necklace. I took the jacket off my shoulders and wrapped it around Sherry's badly damaged arm and tied it in place with the leather tongs that had previously held the Clovis point to my neck. As I completed fixing the last knot I noticed out of the corner of my eye a shrub that seemed to move in my direction. I shuddered, and then I thought I saw another and then a third. It was surreal and uncomfortable. In the dark of night the bushes seemed to be moving in on me. Branches like arms and hands, even faces were almost evident.

Soon I was being nudged aside as the arms emerged from under what appeared to be branches. They were sliding under Sherry. She was being raised up by the small arms of the branches. I was sure that the bushes were moving Sherry up the steep bank. Gil licked her face as she slowly moved away from me.

Sherry began to disappear from my sight as what I saw as bushes and Gil moved her. I was in total darkness alone. The beam of light that came from the flashlight on my head was my only companion. Suddenly I felt very weak.

⅄

In the distance I could hear a voice, "Jake get up, come on." I could feel a warm damp presence on my cheek. I was warm all over. Gradually I began to come to. There I was in my bed in St. John Cave. The Old Man was there and the cat's mug was on my face licking me. Wake up the Old Man said out loud. As I became more aware, I remembered the fight with Rollands. *Did he get the best of me,* I wondered.

"Where is Sherry," I said loudly.

"She is in the hospital in Durango, or Seattle by now." The Old Man said.

"We found her in a cave in Mesa Verde the other night."

"I know I was there," I said.

"Well I don't know about that but I know you have been sleeping for almost two days," the Old Man said.

"What do you mean," I said.

"Don't you remember right after the meeting with Chris you said you were tired and you wanted to lay down?"

"Well um…" I said.

"You missed the wake up and the group, Antonio, myself and Chris got a tip that Sherry was there. We left and followed this guy Kareem Razier to a small Cave and we dug her out."

"I know I was there!" I said.

"Maybe in spirit," the Old Man responded. I could tell by the way he looked at me that he wanted to say more. He did not.

"What about the horses," I asked, "and where are Ieke Rollands and Carlos?"

"We did see a lot of evidence that mustangs had been there. It was strange too that the hoof prints of the mustangs were there and also some obviously domesticated horses, because their prints showed signs of split hooves, you know that mustangs have clear perfectly formed hooves even when living in harsh terrain. Domesticated horses hooves become split and cracked even after a few weeks in the wild. Funny you mention Carlos. He was found early this morning in a bathroom in Seattle."

"What do you mean?" I inquired.

142

KNIGHT JUSTICE

"Well, I guess the news reports that said that Carlos had escaped were not quite correct. There was a lot of confusion and there was an explosion of sorts, I guess the hot water pipes feeding the courtroom broke and people thought that he had escaped by jumping out of a blown out glass. The window was broken and the bars were bent; but nobody could get out that way, the investigators determined. Turns out that was all hysteria. Anyway, old Carlos it seems, ended up in all the confusion, down in the jail restroom in the basement. They found him days later tied to a urinal, fancy that."

"No that is all wrong." I protested.

"Well that is what it must be," the Old Man said.

I noticed two other Knights in the background listening in. I decided I would, for the moment, drop it.

"Now let's get a move on," the Old Man said. "We have to meet a plane in Albuquerque in just over two hours. Take everything with you, you are headed for Seattle."

I jumped out of bed and threw everything I had into my backpack. Minutes later I was headed outside. As I trudged down out the mile long trail to the car the Old Man caught up to me. He was huffing and puffing. A small line of fog was visible on the lower lens of his black rimmed glasses. He put his hand on my shoulder.

"Now you will have to be careful what you say and who you say it to. Things are getting a bit out of control." He said as he tossed my beat up bag in the back seat.

As we pulled out, I had to say it again, "I was there when we rescued Sherry, I couldn't have been dreaming."

The Old Man looked over at me and I saw tension in his eyes as he said, "Are you sure, maybe you *were* dreaming."

"No," I said, "I remember just before I passed out, these bushes were carrying Sherry up the rock cliff."

The Old Man just looked at me as if to say are you sure you want others to hear what you are saying.

The Old Man said, "Bushes?"

It was then I began to get it. The truth was slowly beginning to sink in. But I just could not let it go. I remembered back to some readings I had done about the " little people" of the Cherokees and Zuni's.

Yes, I thought, *If they exist they could have carried Sherry up the hill. The rock people or the Dogwood people or little people. Didn't Jesus say don't forget the little ones?*

Slowly I turned to The Old Man and said, "Have you ever heard of the "Little People?"

He looked at me for a moment and said, "They say that is a legend."

"So you have heard of the "little people" I exclaimed, "They have long hair down to the ground and they live around caves and rocks and they do good and help the sick and poor. And the dogwood trees, have you noticed, the flower is in the shape of a cross?"

"Jake," he said, "now you are headed up to Seattle. Is this story, the one you want to tell the press and everyone? Maybe you ought to think it through. Are you sure that you weren't dreaming. Doesn't that make more sense?"

It was then I became saddened.

"Where is truth in all this," I found myself yelling.

"I think you can trust Razier. Take your lead from him." The Old Man said.

I know I can trust the Old Man with my life but Razier?

As the winding road passed Taos and then Santa Fe I found myself feeling very isolated. I was beginning to feel the real weight of leadership. I had experienced it before as an athlete and as a principal.

To be clear, it is just heavier when people's lives are on the line. That is a fact.

About 40 minutes later we were on the tarmac loading onto the Gulfstream. As the hatch closed I sat down next to a chair that was in a reclined position and under the chair I noticed a small piece of wood that had been sharpened on one end. It was about eight inches long and was attached to a small piece of white fabric. As I looked more closely, I thought I noticed dried blood on the stick. I had seen that kind of thing on Sherry's waist the other evening. I was sure of it. As the small plane started down the runway, I worried that Sherry might be in bad shape. I looked closely at the small drops of dried blood on one arm of the reclined seat.

I wonder what Sherry meant when she said find arrow, Aion or eon or whatever she said just before lights went out for me. I can't seem to let it go. I know she was there and I know what she said.

CHAPTER 34

January 22, 2001, Touch Go

The jet landed at Boeing field and immediately took off. We barely had time to exit the tarmac. A car was already waiting and picked me and the Old Man up. We fought the traffic through downtown and finally we were dropped off at University Hospital. As we walked through the drizzle I had flashes of Sherry's face. She was gaunt and bloody. I shook my head and sighed.

The Old Man patted me on the back and said, "She is gonna be okay Kid you know that."

I nodded yes.

We ended upstairs in the intensive care unit. The head nurse was not letting anyone in to see Sherry.

"Now I know that it is not visiting hours but you have got to let me see her," I said.

The charge nurse finally relented as I had nearly forced my way past her.

I looked in and there she was. Sherry looked to me like a radiant beam of sunlight. Well not quite, she had a tube in her nose and she had bruises all over one side of her face. I could hear in the background the constant beep, beep, and beep of what I knew to be regular sinus rhythm.

"Thank heavens," I said loudly.

I was nearly on top of her now. She slowly turned her head and croaked, "Hi Jake, are you okay?"

I bent over and kissed her on the forehead and she smiled. I could smell her hair and it smelled just like I remembered; the sweet scent of Sherry. My heart was racing and I barely noticed the charge nurse pulling on my back.

"Now she has had a very rough go and I am sure you don't want to make matters worse!" The nurse directed in a kind yet firm manner.

"You're right," I said.

Sherry slowly moved her left hand to me and I grabbed it and held tight as I looked at her. It was that moment; I knew that I was in love with her. To me she seemed like an angel. I sat with her for the next ten hours. She mainly slept. I thought I could see a smile on her bruised face and that made me happy. From time to time a visiting Dr. stopped in. I was in the company of as many as three plain cloths guards posted in the area. They said nothing, nor did I.

At about 2:00 AM, I inched my way to the door looking back at Sherry all the while.

As I walked out of the room I said, "keep good care of her," to the two Seattle police officers posted outside her door. They looked very sleepy.

The Old Man was sitting cross legged just outside the nurses' station in the waiting area. I said, "Let's go see my kids." He looked up, smiled and nodded. As we headed down the cold sterile hall, I said nothing to the Old Man and he said nothing to me. We made our way to the elevator. Once on the main floor, we walked by the newsstand and I grabbed the weekend Seattle Star newspaper.

We got to the parking lot and jumped into the car. Once out of the parking garage, we headed south. We took the exit and went west on the 520. Heading south on I-5, we passed downtown Seattle on the right. We drove over the I-90 Bridge and up to my folk's home.

A note on the door said, "Come on in, Shh, kids are asleep. A room is ready for your friend in the basement."

I took The Old Man down, showed him around and went up to my room. As I crawled into bed, the clock said 3:00 AM.

The next morning I was awakened by Katy my daughter. A quick glance at the clock told me it was 9:00 AM. She ran into the room and dove into my bed. Sam, on the other hand, was a horse of a different color. He did not look at me during breakfast and did not speak to me. He reminded me of the cost; the cost to me personally. Yet I could not help but think about the military families and families of foreign contractors that are split up at a moment's notice not seeing each other again for months, years or God forbid, never again. I shed a tear as I watched Sam gradually warm up to me. I was now fully engaged in the life that I was choosing. It not only hurt me, it hurt the kids. Yet, I knew I was engaged in important work that had to be done. I was going to do it to the highest level.

Later in the day, I had a chance to look over the Seattle Star newspaper I had picked up at the Hospital. There on the front page were my constant companions. The headline read; Sherry Sips Soup in Hospital. It told of how according to Kareem Razier he had seen her taken months earlier and followed and eventually foiled the plot to extort money from the authorities in return for Sherrie's safe return.

I yelled at the paper, "That is so much horse pucky." According to Razier's rendition, the finger was pointed squarely at Carlos Castilano and amazingly Ieke Rollands, former Superintendent of the Seattle Schools. The article stated that Rollands abruptly resigned from his position for personal reasons.

Quoting Razier, reporter Ruth Thaif wrote, "Rollands paid me to watch Ms. Paul since she was a masquerading teacher and possibly up to no good." The article suggested Ieke Rollands promised to pay $50,000 for her safe return. Razier was quoted as saying, "I tracked Rollands down to an underground structure at Fort Worden just outside Port Townsend Washington. The underground abandoned munitions cave contains a treasure trove of Sherry Paul's items and articles. This guy is sick. I have no idea why the authorities held me. It is Rollands they want not me. And I have the taped conversations to prove it."

The story continued "…also of interest is, Mr. Jake Rader, former Principal of Cedarvale High School who disappeared from his post days after Ms. Paul's abduction. Key to this investigation will be Ms. Paul as soon as she is well enough to be interviewed. She is now in protective custody in an undisclosed location. It is rumored that Jake Rader is in Washington DC."

It also mentioned that Carlos Castilano who previously was thought to have escaped from the King County Superior Court was found duct taped to a urinal in the basement of the Superior Court building. Ieke Rollands was rumored to have discovered Castilano and Razier in the restroom.

In a related piece, "Conroll Bas Boyd, a convicted criminal and former Army Sniper," was said to have been tentatively identified.

"His remains were discovered in an isolated area an hour's drive west of Fort Warden, Washington. Fort Warden is the location where Kareem Razier said Sherry Paul was held. The body was found a few miles off of Blue Mountain Road in a wilderness area not far from Port Angeles, Washington." The article also suggested that a partially dismembered body appeared to have been torn apart by a mountain lion. One unattached forearm, had an x and crescent tattooed on it. The tracks of the lion seemed to indicate a female of less than one hundred pounds. There were no scrapes or male markings in the area. Boyd served as an attaché to General Ieke Rollands in Vietnam.

"Rollands," it said, "was, not available for comment and had not been contacted by the authorities at the time of printing." I was shocked and shaken by the articles. I immediately asked the Old Man who was just coming upstairs for the first time, "what is the meaning of this?"

I shook the paper at him.

"Did you know about this?" I asked as I continued to wave the paper in his face.

"Now Jake let's calm down a bit."

"Well did you?" I repeated.

"That's what I was telling you; things are getting a bit dicey. But help Razier to the degree you can. Keep in mind that a report is nothing more than a report until the evidence is proven in court. In the meantime you can help Sherry recover. Let's not talk to her about any of this now. You know what I am saying Jake?"

"Don't worry, I don't plan to. Am I going to get a police visit?" I quizzed.

The Old Man drew in a long slow breath and said, "Jake I know you will handle this well. Ya know, this is why you were trained. Now just keep delivering the goods. As you white eyes say you are the mail man." He laughed.

Then Katy burst into the room jumped into my lap and asked, "Daddy are you going to jail?"

"No honey," I said, "you don't have to worry about that."

I gave her a long and strong hug.

CHAPTER 35

January 26, 2001, Shock Awe

I opened the passenger car door as the Old Man slowly slid out of the seat. He swung his small satchel over his back.

"Well son," he said, "It's your game and yours alone, now make us proud."

I looked at him for a moment as he reached out of his pocket. In his hand, glistening in the dreary Seattle mist, were five small, golden coins.

"Here are a few pfennigs to get you by." He joked.

As he lifted his hand towards mine, I could not help but notice the date of 1596 on one of the coins. He casually dropped them one at a time into my out stretched hand. As I saw the coins I suspected that they were part of the treasure taken off Malta by the Knights of St. John. The sun momentarily broke through the clouds as he turned and then walked towards the sparkling white jet plane. *I am going to miss that old savage.*

I stood for a few more minutes as the Gulfstream taxied, surged down the runway and then jumped off the ground like a fleet young pony. I slowly walked back to my car reflecting on this unique and small friend. I got in and started the engine with a lump in my throat.

As I drove the short distance down I-5 to University Hospital, I repressed the feeling of being responsible for the entire nightmare and yet I knew I was up to my eyeballs in the rescue and the protection of Sherry. Clearly I knew too much of Ieke Rollands and his activity. I knew I would face him again and soon. I was beginning to feel that I was not alone and it felt so good. I still shuddered to think about Sherry's diet of pinion nuts and tainted water.

How could she survive that terrible treatment, I thought as I drove along.

She was about to be released and I was very happy about that. I knew that her work was not over. Sherry had agreed to spend some additional recovery time at my parents', you know getting to know Sam and Katy and stuff. Sam was still not talking to me much and I hoped that Sherry might help me get to him a bit. I pulled into the parking garage and secured the car. I nearly forgot to lock the door as I jogged into the main entrance. I noticed that my head did not hurt when I jogged.

I had been having slight headaches ever since my altercation with Ieke Rollands that evening a few weeks earlier at Mesa Verde. I also noticed that the cut on the back of my head was not sore to the touch even with my Mariners baseball cap turned backwards. As I passed by the hospital convenience store, I bought a rose.

Nice touch, I thought as I pushed the elevator button.

I nearly sprung into the elevator as a senior couple scowled at me. I pushed the fifth floor button and looked straight ahead as I felt them stare at my behind.

The bell rang and the door opened as I turned to the couple and said, "Have an excellent day."

I rushed down the hall and smiled as I passed by the nurse's station for the last time, I hoped. It was just five minutes past 12: 00 PM Sherry was to be getting out any time after noon. She was becoming a very strong light in my life. I had spent the last week noon to 9:00

PM at my parents' home with the kids and the late evenings and mornings with Sherry. She had provided me with the learnings she had received in the cave. They were profound. She had me, bagged bound and boxed.

As I burst into the room there he was standing right in front of me. He had what must have been four dozen red roses in his arms and he was handing them to Sherry. I looked down at my small slightly wilted rose and restrained the impulse to hide it. I just knew my face was bright red. Not red like a little pinkish cream but full on blood red.

Ieke turned to me and said, "Hey sport how's it goin?"

"I am well," I managed to eke out.

I thought, *how can this guy even face her, he knows I know he nearly killed her and he is standing here like nothing ever happened? What about us didn't he and I have a knock down drag out down on the mesa?*

He then turned to Sherry and said, "Come here Kitty, give me a big hug!"

Sherry got up and hugged him. I seemed to me that the embrace was five minutes or longer. Finally I thought I saw Sherry push away. Anyway, by now I was sure my face was purple, but I did not care, I was mad.

Ieke said, "Now please consider my offer; you can use my entire guest suite as long as you want. I mean it."

"Thank you Ieke really," Sherry said. She sat down on the end of the bed looking a bit pale.

"Jake will you ask the nurse for a vase for your flower," she said with a forced smile.

"Oh all right," I said automatically.

When I returned He was gone.

I wanted to remind her about that evening in Mesa Verde but the Old Man's words rang in my ears "Let's not trouble her with this."

Sherry was still sitting on the end of the bed. She had her head in her hands and acting like she was not feeling well.

"Sherry what is it?" I asked.

"Just a little light headed," she said with a smile.

I turned, ran out of the room and called for the nurse. When the nurse arrived she said, "Jake what have you done?" The nurse walked over and took Sherry's pulse. I could tell by the look on the nurse's face that something was wrong. Something was very wrong.

I looked at her in disbelief and said, "What are you talking about?"

The nurse said, "I leave you alone with her and I come back and she is not well." I glanced down at Sherry's breakfast tray and noticed that Sherry had not touched her food.

"Sherry," I said, "you have not eaten maybe that is the problem."

"I am just a little dizzy," she said.

"What have you had to eat today," the nurse said.

Sherry replied, "I just had a few sips of this coffee that Ieke gave me and Dr. Adams, from Seabucks."

I grabbed the coffee and took a small sip.

"This is sour, I said, "It smells like rancid almonds." The old nurse with silver shoulder length hair had just taken Sherry's pulse and I could tell from her response that she believed me. The nurse laid down the blood pressure cuff she was about to attach to Sherry's arm and took a small whiff of the coffee.

"I agree," she said.

Sherry said, "I am very dizzy."

She laid down in her bed. The nurse pushed an alarm button on the arm of Sherry's bed. Immediately the room was filled with hospital personnel. The next thing I knew, they were wheeling Sherry out of the room.

I heard one say" I don't like those arrhythmias. And her breathing is shallow and halting."

"I grabbed the coffee cup and handed it with two hands like it
was a precious gift to one of the doctors. I said, "Have this analyzed
and you will find what is troubling Sherry."

I noticed out of the corner of my eye that the officer assigned to
Sherry was already on the phone.

I yelled, "Follow me!" to the officer as I ran out of the room.

I bounded down the stairs two steps at a time with the officer
right behind.

As I reached the parking garage I noticed Ieke Rollands inside a
late model Lexus just pulling out of the parking garage gate. I ran to
my car. I said, "Get in," to the officer as I pushed open the passenger
side door.

The car was already moving in reverse as he jumped in. I gunned
it and we were off. I pulled right through the toll booth without slow-
ing down. The young kid inside just looked as we squealed past. As
we exited the garage I could see Rolland's car stopped at the light just
before the 520 ramp. I guided the car in and out of traffic. We made
our way close to Rolland's Lexus. Rolland's car bolted and crossed
the intersection against the red light just missing an oncoming green
Toyota. I swerved around the Toyota and gunned it. Rolland's car was
headed west on the 520 when we pulled to within two hundred yards.
The officer was already screaming at his radio.

He said, "We are in pursuit of a south bound Red Lexus, license
IEKE02U on I-5 just past the I-90 interchange; requesting backup."

I heard the dispatcher in the background say, "what is your
emergency?"

The officer yelled, "We are after an attempted murder suspect
and he is dangerous."

I looked down and noticed the speedometer needle edging past 100 mph as the officer said, "Jake you had better be right on this one."

I had, on repeated occasions warned him that Rolland's should not be trusted. This was the first time the officer had taken me seriously.

I could not help but wonder what had changed. *Maybe now he'll believe me?* The little Chevy began to shudder.

"I can't keep up with him," I said.

"You are doing great," he said as we flew past the Michigan Avenue exit. Rollands took the Boeing airport exit increasing his distance from us to a quarter mile or so. We followed in traffic barely able to see the red Lexus well ahead of us.

"He is headed for Boeing field," I said as I saw him turn off towards the east side.

As the officer radioed the dispatcher, I was now convinced that he was headed to Boeing field, I noticed him turn down through a set of warehouses. I followed.

As we screeched into the old Horizon Air terminal, Rollands was jogging towards a Cessna 172 that was already beginning its taxi. As the door of the small four seater turned broadside to our location I spotted the tail number: N3794N. I read the numbers back to the officer as he repeated the numbers to dispatch.

I heard him say, "Correct that is November 379er-4 November."

I briefly entertained the notion of crashing through the chain-link fence and chasing the plane down the runway. I then realized, this is real not like some Hollywood thriller. Moments later we saw the plane ascending as it disappeared over the horizon. We drove the short distance to the tower. I jumped out of the car. The motor was still running. I hustled up the stairs. I tried to barge into the flight controller's station. The door was locked and the supervisor responded negatively to my beating on the door. After a brief and heated explanation, we were granted an audience with the air traffic controller.

I said, "Where is the Cessna tail number N3794N headed?"

"Sir," he said, "there is no Cessna with that number. The number you just gave me is for a Mooney M20F Executive or Beechcraft Bonanza also known as the Dr. Killer. We call that plane, the day the music died."

"What do you mean?" I quizzed looking at him strangely?

"That, my friend is the tail number of the plane in which Buddy Holly was killed."

I thought to myself, *is this some kind of joke.* Then I thought, *our deranged friend did just attempt to kill Sherry and her doctor?*

I looked the controller straight in the eye and said, "listen buddy, we need to know what plane just took off and where it is headed."

"Well the only plane to take of was a Cessna tail number CC DAB; and no one filed a flight plan. That would be a plane registered in Chile because of the CC letters on the tail section.

"What does that mean," the officer said from behind me?

"That means the plane could go anywhere and might be difficult to track."

"Can you find it?" I asked.

"I doubt it; the plane took off, made a sharp turn to the west and dropped below radar visibility."

"Is that to suggest it may have crashed?" I asked.

"No most likely they are flying low along the bay possibly out the straights or down south Puget Sound by Gig Harbor or even south to Chehalis. In any case, there are numerous mountains and small fields they might have landed in or they may have just kept going. It's hard to say."

We walked back to the car dejected and upset only to find four black and whites sitting in the parking lot. I told the officer I was headed back to the hospital.

He turned from his conversation with one of the other cops and said, "You might like to know that Sherry is doing better but the doctor. who treated her, these past few weeks is not. He died this afternoon and from preliminary reports he may have died of cyanide poisoning."

"That is what I guessed," I said, "Rollands laced the Seabucks coffee with ground up apple seeds and or cherry pits.

It doesn't take too many baked ground up pips to do the trick. I had better get back to Sherry."

The officer continued, "Let me know what you find on our mister Rollands."

CHAPTER 36

JANUARY 28, 2001, MENDING WELL

I spent the next two days at University Hospital by Sherry's side. She was doing better. Dr. Tragor told her that she drank just enough apple seed laced coffee to make her sick. Her Dr. Adams did not fare so well. He was gone. The autopsy showed cyanide poisoning of the same chemical makeup found in Sherry's coffee. Sherry was lucky, I had arrived just in time to prevent her from ingesting enough to kill her.

"How are you feeling?" I asked Sherry.

"Much better," she said.

The medical staff had prevented Jes Utic of the Seattle Police detectives from interviewing Sherry because, she, until the last day, was still confused. Now I was not sure what they meant. Nor did I want to know. She had been through an ordeal of unbelievable proportions and I was sure she would have to handle it in her own good time.

"Jake I am so excited we are going to get out of this place I did not want to be interviewed here. I don't have to meet with the police until tomorrow." She said. "I have an Idea; let's stop by the pier on the way to your parents' and we can watch the boats on the water. It seems like an eternity since I have been able to smell the fresh air and feel the sun on my face." Sherry said.

"Great thinking," I said. Frankly anything would be better than an hour ride across the bridge sitting in traffic and wondering how to begin a more normal existence.

"We had better get on the road if we want to do that," I said impatiently.

The nurse rolled in an old chrome wheel chair with a blue vinyl seat. I plucked the now blackened and saggy rose out of the small vase. It had been sitting in the corner unnoticed for days. To me it was a reminder that life is fleeting and all I could do was cherish and celebrate it. Sherry was wearing the new clothes I brought for her, a down filled jacket, a simple white blouse, blue wrangler jeans and Nike Air Joggers. She smiled as she looked back to see the dozens of wilted roses lying on the counter. Then she looked up at the one in my hand. She grabbed my arm and winked. I smiled back. The nurse wheeled Sherry out of the hospital room, down the hall and into the waiting elevator. When we reached the ground floor, I jogged ahead and got the car. As I arrived at the service entrance I noticed sun-flower seeds all over the passenger side seat.

I jumped out of the car opened the passenger door and said, "your ride awaits madam."

Sherry slid into the car and rested her casted left wrist on the center console. She didn't notice or at least didn't mention the seeds she sat on.

I thanked the nurse and hopped to the driver side door. As I slid in, I asked Sherry, "it's finally over are you ready to relax for awhile?"

"Well," she said, "after the testimony and all I will be much better."

I pulled onto the 520 bridge extension heading west. I felt a sense of relief and excitement. Months of gut-wrenching trauma, isolation and anxiety were finally behind us and the storm clouds were beginning to break. Yet in the back of my mind were the embers of the truth. Ieke Rollands was still out there and he was going to be taunting us. Yet on the whole, at that very moment, I was indeed very happy.

CHAPTER 37

MOMENTS LATER, PIER JOY

Five minutes later we slowly drove along below the Alaskan Way Viaduct looking for a spot close to Ivar's fish bar. I stopped the car just under the concrete and steel columns that made up the road support just above us. As we were getting out an old man wearing a tattered flannel shirt and saggy blue jeans stuck out his hand and said, "Brother can you spare some change?"

I stepped between the guy and Sherry just as a big green Washington State ferry blew its horn.

Sherry grabbed her ears with a smile and said loudly, "That is truly a wonderful sound isn't it Jake?"

"Well," I said, "I like that better than the sound of heart monitors and oxygen sensors."

I turned back as I reached into my pocket and pulled out a free burger certificate from the local MacDonald's and an invite card to the Summit feast. I handed them to the pan handler. He looked at the free burger certificate and tossed it onto the ground as we waked on. As I looked back I saw him looking carefully at the invitation. I hoped that he would follow the directions on the card. These would lead him to the gathering at the summit club. I knew he could receive love and support in that group, if he would only take the first steps. I had to refocus might thoughts as Sherry continued.

"That didn't bother me. I guess it's a matter of volume. I like big sounds in big spaces." Sherry said as we crossed slowly in front of an approaching nineteen hundreds vintage red and green street car.

As we made our way across the street Sherry said, "Jake isn't it beautiful. The setting sun on the water, I am so thankful we are here together."

She grabbed my hand with her casted palm and somehow it just felt right. Even though the rays of the sun were barely visible through the Seattle maritime sky I was feeling the joy that I sensed in Sherry. She was different somehow and I liked it.

There was no room inside the diner on Pier 54 so we decided to eat right on the board walk. As we walked towards the rustic covered eating area just above the tidelands I looked down into the seaweed filled slimy green water. It lapped against the oil stained pilings. Some logs and kelp swayed slowly on the surface. I wondered, just for that instant what Carlos and his buddy must have felt tied to a driftwood raft not far from that very spot. It had been less than a year. My eyes happened to catch the sun as it sparkled on the water of the bay. I had to agree with Sherry it was in fact beautiful.

As we sat under the heaters, smelling the salty air I prayed to myself, *Thank you for the precious gift of life and for the wonders of nature you show us every day.*

"I agree," Sherry said.

I looked at her scarred face without makeup and wondered, *am really looking at an angel?* It seemed to me that I was indeed.

Just as I finished my thought, she leaned up to me, looked me in the eyes, tilted her head slightly and kissed me on the lips. Her lips were warm and soft but all I could taste was fried cod and salt. Just then I became overwhelmed. I thought I might well up with tears, but, instead I just burst out laughing. The thought of kissing a salty cod fish was all I could take. I laughed so loud that the couple, bundled up in a blanket at the next table looked over as if to say, "You two are out of control."

I shot a quick glance back as I said, "kids these days you can't take 'em anywhere."

This got a smile from the gal while the guy just remained stoically non -emotive.

I reached over and zipped up Sherry's jacket as I felt the cold evening sea breeze coming off shore and knew that she had to be getting cold. I was becoming very protective but I gave myself a pass because of all the trauma of the past few weeks.

"Funny, how a few months make a difference isn't it Jake?" Sherry asked.

I just smiled, but deep down I knew that things had changed and we were not just a couple of kids out on a date. I also knew there was little either of us could do about it. I shuddered to think about the realities both of us would be facing during the next few weeks. I was not looking forward to the rainy days ahead.

"I am happy Jake are you?"

"We have got to get you home," I said as I was becoming increasingly embarrassed at the direction things were heading. Not that I was minding it at all.

⚓

It was nearly 8:00 PM when we arrived back in Issaquah. We received welcomed hugs and kisses from the kids and my mom and dad. At that very moment life felt just right. I walked Sherry down to the room that mom had prepared for her.

"Sherry walked to the door, turned and said, "Jake thank you, I know all you have done for me and I do appreciate it, even the rose."

I laughed as tears rolled down my splotchy red cheeks. I glanced down at the wilting flower, grabbed her hand and drew her close. Our gaze was fixed and our eyes nearly touched. I was dizzy as my head moved closer to her and she pulled me tight with her good arm. We held each other in a warm embrace for an instant and then as I felt her warm lips touch mine, I knew I did not want to let go.

"Jake is there anything Sherry needs?" It was my mother singing from the top of the stairs.

For a brief moment I did not flinch. *Yes mom we need a bit of privacy.* As Sherry moved back I whispered, "I Love you Sherry Paul."

She whispered, "I know!"

Then I replied in a loud voice, "I think she is just fine."

"I will see you tomorrow," I said to Sherry, as I reluctantly walked towards the stairs.

I completed my kisses and hugs to the kids who were already in their beds upstairs. Katy prayed: "Please God, keep my Daddy safe and help Sherry, she looks like she needs it."

After our good night prayers, I left them again. I was glad that this time it was just for the night.

I really did not want to go home to my cold and lonely home that was filled with the visages of the past. As I got into my car I could not help but think about the future. *Tomorrow, Sherry and I will face the detectives,* I remembered. We both will face the harsh reality of the total mess we were part of. As I drove up to my house, I could not help consider that but for divine presence I was still very alone. This home and all that I had worked for in my short life had been turned upside down and now it was by my choice.

I stepped in and looked around the house. It was cold and lifeless. I walked over to the bookcase. There it was, on the right hand side of the fire place. I picked up the last picture taken of my wife and the kids. She was so skinny and frail. Katy and Sam looked so young.

They really have grown in the past year. I had not felt that wave of loss in over a month.

Now here it is again.

Just one small tear flowed down my cheek and onto the picture as if to say that's it. You have really done it this time. I was now facing a real psychological assault. Not only had I lost my first wife, but, due to my own choice, I was losing my kids. Finally I was hooking up with an old friend and I was moving on. Slowly I carried the picture back to my room like the fragile treasure it was and sat it on the night stand. I just pulled the bedspread over me, shoes and all.

As I was about to drift off, Sherry's words came back to me in a dreamy voice. "Jake you must find Ariel Aion."

What possibly could she have meant?

CHAPTER 38

THE NEXT DAY, QUESTIONS ANSWERS

I took the 405 south as I made my way back to my parents' house in Issaquah. Thank goodness the traffic was lighter than usual. I arrived early. As I exited the car I noticed my watch read 7:00 AM. I walked up the half flight of stairs that lead to the main living quarters. As I ascended the last stair I heard voices coming from the kitchen. I thought that Sherry would still be downstairs, possibly asleep. Instead she was helping out in the kitchen.

"Jake, I am glad you finally decided to show up," Sherry said with a smile.

Mom was setting the last of the dishes on the table. Dad was at his favorite kitchen spot. He was cooking omelets, his masterpiece, possibly his only, breakfast dish. Katy and Sam were not yet up.

"We are due at the Seattle Police Station at 9:30 AM." Sherry said.

"I know, and I don't feel well prepared, do you?" I asked.

"Jake you are prepared, that's what your training was all about..."

"How do you know?" I asked.

"Didn't you get the memo?" Sherry chortled.

"Chris told me," Sherry said after a long pause.

"When did you see him?" I questioned.

"When he brought me to the Hospital in Seattle."

"He brought you to the Hospital?"

Out of the corner of my eye I could see Mom's eyes focused intently on our conversation.

"Please pass the orange juice," I said, as I attempted to divert from the conversation.

"I think we will need to get on the road right away," I said, as I knew there were important matters to discuss. "Plus," I said, "we are going to be in traffic. Our typical fifteen minute drive will likely take an hour."

As we got into the car we were greeted by arms and hands moving in unison from the upstairs window. Sam, Katy, Mom and Dad were waiving vigorously as they knelt from the couch above.

I spared no time as we pulled from the driveway. "Sherry," I said, "what are you going to say about the cave to the police? Because you know they will be all over the facts. Razier says you were in a cave in Fort Warden while Rollands has asserted you were in New Mexico. The Old Man told me that I should support Razier and Razier is not correct."

"Well," Sherry said, "don't believe all you read in the newspapers."

"What do you mean?" I asked.

"Jake just answer the questions and you will be fine."

"I plan to but it's you I am concerned about."

"Me? I am just fine Mister Rader!"

"Okay, so what is this Arrow, Alien or elon or whatever you wanted me to find?" I asked, "it kept me awake last night."

"Jake now that you are a Knight, you must learn more than just the disciplines of the body and mind and the ability to wage war.

More importantly, you have to develop your spirit. I have been saved by this knowledge."

"Where do I find this? Can you be clearer?" I asked.

"You will be found if you really want to. Do you want to be found Jake?"

"You know I am in this for the duration," I said quickly.

I hit the brakes hard as the traffic on the I-90 Bridge came to a complete stop. The traffic moved slowly all the way to the I-5 exit where we headed north. A few minutes later we reached the Seattle Police Department parking garage. As Sherry and I approached the main entrance I was surprised to find a crowd of at least 20 people gathered there. As we moved through the crowd reporters and camera people began yelling.

"Hey Jake did you really save Sherry?"

"Sherry, what is life like in a cave?"

"What will you tell the police today?"

As we pressed by the group we did not answer questions but I could tell Sherry was upset especially when I heard a TV reporter Yell, "Well do you love him? Do ya love Jake, Sherry?" Fortunately we were now inside the building and I asked the stern and matronly looking receptionist for Jes Utic.

"Straight ahead and to the right," the gruff lady said as she pointed with her left hand. As we started in through the maze of blue shirted officers, I could tell that many stopped to look as we made our way past the desks.

Jes greeted us as we made our way to the glass walled interrogation areas. He held out his hand.

"You must be Jake," he said as he shot me his hand.

"Sherry you are as pretty as I imagined you and a bit taller I guess." He said as he smiled. He had a disarming way about him. I reminded myself to be careful because these types can cause trouble.

Sherry just smiled and said, "You look older than I thought you might look."

He laughed out loud as he pulled out a chair for Sherry and pointed to one on the other side for me.

He sat down and jumped right into the matter.

"I am sure that you and Jake have heard and read a great deal on your ordeal Sherry. Let me begin to straighten things out for you. First off we know that you were imprisoned in New Mexico. The whole story of the Fort Warden cave was just a way to get Ieke Rollands to admit that he was in Mesa Verde the evening you were rescued. In addition we found a stash of great evidence in Fort Warden. Based upon Kareem Razier's statement and that of Carlos Castilano, Rollands is going to be put away for a long time."

"Have you tracked him down?" I asked.

"Well no but we have evidence that his plane was spotted in Chiapas, Mexico on the ground. We think he is headed to Chile because of the ownership and registration of the Cessna. Jake your quick action allowed us to get the call numbers on the plane early and that was absolutely necessary to tracking the plane down. When we reviewed the tape of the plane taking off from Boeing field we noticed that as it reached about 200 feet the white numbers tore off the side and floated back to the runway. Then it was easy to track the plane back to the original location and fortunately when it landed early in the morning, it had the Chile registration tail number. We are working with partners in Central America and we will get him.

It seems that the cave in Fort Warden had been used by the Seattle School District for an outdoor survival course for leadership staff. We now know this based on Razier's written testimony that he and Castilano and others were trained by Rollands himself at the underground gun emplacements at Fort Warden. I think Razier will get a lighter sentence as he has been a cooperative witness. Anyway, had it not been for you Jake, Sherry would have been left down that canyon to die."

"By the way, Sherry, how did you get up to the road after Jake found you?" Utic asked.

Sherry responded, "I don't know, I was not with it, I think the only humanly possible way was that Jake carried me up out of there."

"Jake did you carry her out?"

"If I did I don't remember," I said. "By the way, where are you getting this information?" I asked.

"Rollands told us."

"What else did he say?" I asked.

"He said he and Christian brought Sherry back to Seattle since they were not confident of the medical attention Sherry might receive in northwestern New Mexico."

"Did you talk to Christian or someone else to confirm?" I demanded.

"We had special agents on the ground there too. I don't even know this Christian. "

"Wait just a minute; are you saying that there were Seattle police in New Mexico?" I asked.

"I'm not saying that." Utic said.

"All-right; things are getting a little fishy here," I said.

"Then why is Ieke the bad guy?" Sherry asked.

"You have got to be kidding me, Sherry do you remember why you had to spend a week longer in the hospital?"

"Sorry Jake I don't, let's talk later."

"Who were these agents anyway? Who might they have been? I was there, there were no other agents," I said with conviction.

"Jake where was this exactly and who else was there?" Utic querried.

I was beginning to think that I was being led into a trap of some kind so I decided to clam up.

"I don't really know because I passed out."

Sherry glanced at me and gave me a hint of a smile.

"That is what I thought," Utic said.

"By the way, did you know that they did find a computer chip in a financial clerk's office at Cedarvale High School?" Jes Utic wondered.

"And how much damage was done?" I asked.

"That is a matter for those outside my pay grade to answer." Utic replied.

"Sherry, I have one more question, was it Razier who took you hostage?" Utic asked.

"I will have to say yes, he and others." Sherry Replied.

"I think we are done here," Utic said.

I was upset and more confused than ever. As we walked out of the police office somehow I knew this was going to take a while to understand.

Just as we approached the steps a Channel Five reporter asked, "Well is Rollands guilty?"

Sherry said, "Ariel knows, find the face, and you will find the answers to everything." Sherry's smile stretched across her beautiful, slightly pale face.

Reporters and people holding cameras shouted questions as we walked by.

"Who is this Ariel?"

"Where can we find her?"

"Do you know her very well?"

As we pushed through the others I just looked at Sherry. She smiled back.

CHAPTER 39

FIVE MONTHS LATER, RISK REWARD

As Sherry was recuperating, she took up quarters with my parents. Fortunately in addition to the three bedrooms upstairs they maintained an entire suite downstairs. This suite provided the perfect spot for Sherry. There was a small bar that doubled as a kitchen. She however ate more with the family upstairs than downstairs, that is when she was not out with me. Sherry still walked with a limp.

She had some difficulty ascending and descending stairs. She did not mind the difficulties. Living there with my folks allowed her to really get to know my kids. It was heartening to see how taken Sam was with Sherry. I noticed that she also, was quite the fan of Sam. The benefit to me was that I had time and the desire to get my own half abandoned place in better order. I jumped at the chance and began the process of cleaning up the house and fixing up all the pieces of a neglected home. I even helped as a hired man cleaned the gutters. The gutters had two years' cedar duff in them. Don't misunderstand, I still had obligations. For example I had the dubious privilege of testifying in the Castiano trial. Nearly all of my testimony was thrown out as hearsay. I did tell the court that I watched Sherry leave the gym with Cazided. That was about it. There is a new investigation into his whereabouts.

In addition, I spent as much time as possible with the kids; you know, the zoo, the park and school performances. I grew weary of "home rehab" so I planned another family outing mainly as an escape. I wanted Sherry to take the trip with us. She agreed that we should take the kids to Seattle Center since they did not have to be in school. I was required to be in a meeting in Seattle. Sherry and the kids planned to catch up with me that afternoon. Unfortunately that didn't work. She had dizzy spells and didn't feel she should be driving with the kids.

She still wanted to join Katy and Sam on the Seattle Center trip. That was all good. However, the previous day, Sherry told me that as soon as her headaches were gone she would be ready to get back into it. That meant a rigorous training schedule. She was now able to walk without much of a limp and she had been cleared to start an exercise routine. It also meant she was thinking about work again.

"Jake you can be my personal trainer," she joked at dinner the night before.

Somehow I knew it was not a joke. For the past week I was having a nagging feeling that the kids would not be too excited to see us leave again. Yet I knew that with the life I chose I would not be available to stay with them. Especially now, since Ieke Rollands and a few of his lunatics were still on the run. Besides, things where not safe for Sherry or me. Until Ieke Rollands was apprehended, I had to do as much with the kids as possible. Sherry had bonded with both of the kids. My parents liked her and that was good for me. Frankly it would have been easier just to call it quits right then and there. I even thought I might be able to get my real job back. That was my fantasy.

In the real world, I knew that you can't go back, at least not the same way you came.

I was committed and there was no turning back. I knew also deep down, as long as Ieke Rollands was still on the run our life would not be normal. I also realized that I did not want a "normal life". I liked the excitement. Besides I was already spending a large amount of time on Rollands. Sherry didn't even know how much time I was spending on Ieke. I secretly read all the reports on the progress of the investigation. I had met with Jes Utic a couple of times. I was frustrated because there was little on Ieke's whereabouts. It was like Ieke Rollands had just disappeared into thin air.

Today was the day to confront the moment of truth with the kids. I had to find the right time to let the kids know that we would shortly be on the road again. As I rushed back from my meeting with Jes Utic, I knew that today was the day to let the kids know.

"Sam and Katy are you guys ready to go?" I yelled. The kids ran down the stairs, out onto the porch and jumped in the back of the car. We drove the 30 minutes to the Seattle Center and parked. We walked the few short blocks to the Pacific Science Center. I bought a family ticket and we went in. Sherry was tired so we sat in the Math Discovery area.

At that moment I was sitting on a small bench about 30 feet from Sam. He was intently watching the demonstration. It was cool. Ping pong balls were dropped into a clear paneled box just slightly larger than the width of a ping pong table. Each ball rolled down a tube one at a time. When a ball came to the center at the top of a peg board inside the box, it started to hit evenly spaced wooden pegs. The balls randomly bounced off the evenly spaced pegs. One ball came to rest at the top of the column of balls that had previously been dropped. Over time, the columns of balls formed what is called a bell curve or normal distribution. Some fell directly to the bottom barely touching a peg. Others bounced hitting many pegs as they continued down. There were many more balls that found their way to the center of the box then the outside. It reminded me of life.

Isn't it strange how life seems to be for us like the balls? We bounce from here to there in what appears to be a random pattern. But in the end there is a nearly perfect order that comes when we see the big picture. Every once in awhile someone bounces way to the outside for what appears to be no reason at all. It might be a speck of dust that makes the difference. It might be the slickness of the ball. Who knows why but not all the balls fall into the same column. Neither do we. We all choose to go in the direction we are heading or we change direction without notice. In the end, it is not random at all. It is the pattern of life. It is normal.

I can really use this with the kids, I thought, *each of us can pick a ball to watch. Likely the balls will end up in different columns.*

That was just the example I needed to explain to Katy and Sam why Sherry and I needed to leave. We were bouncing down a different way than we may have wanted or planned. But in the end we all would be alright.

As chance would have it, I needed to go to the restroom. I told Sam to wait right there. I did not notice the shady looking character standing to the side of Sam. I was excited I had found a way to talk about the twists and turns of life. This was a great way to have our little yet big, discussion. As I walked in the restroom door, I thought I heard a female voice say "go back". Rather than continue in I headed back out. I was moving with a sense of urgency. As I walked back out of the door, I saw this character head toward Sam.

You have got to be kidding me!

Just as I was about to use this great little demo to explain to the kids why I had to go away again, I was forced back into a chase. All of a sudden this guy grabbed Sam and took off. He must have been waiting there and watching for me to leave. I saw him start down the stairs. I sprang to immediate action and headed out in his direction.

I yelled at Sherry, "Ieke Rollands". That was the code we were to use if there ever was a problem. She jumped up and headed out. Sherry almost ran down the stairs. Her limp was barely noticeable. Katy was just behind her. I jumped over the concrete half wall and swung to the floor below like a gymnast dismounting from a high bar. The guy with a near eastern look ran with a slight limp. He carried Sam over his shoulder. Sam was kicking his legs and swinging his arms.

I heard Sam yell, "Get him Dad!" Sam was screaming at the top of his lungs.

I caught up to them as the perp dropped Sam and continued out the door. Once he was outside he bounded down some concrete stairs knocking a popcorn machine over in my path. I leapt over the machine and down the flight of four stairs. I caught him by the neck and swung him around slamming him to the pavement. The two of us hit the ground and rolled to a stop right near the international fountain steps. He took a swipe at me with a large knife he pulled from his jacket. The blade sliced open my shirt. I yanked his arm backward and around into a "come along" as a Seattle officer on a bike rode up. The guy had already dropped the knife. He was arrested on the spot. I ran to Sherry, Katy and Sam.

Now half crying and half mad, Sam looked at me and said, "Dad don't leave me again, will you?"

I just grabbed him into my arms and hugged him. So much for my great plan! As the police led the attacker away, I realized the bare knuckle facts of life.

We were now into the new phase. What do we do about the kids? They were not safe and we could do little to change that cold hard fact. I had planned to take Sherry out to dinner anyway so I thought it might be a good chance to debrief the day. I was a bit nervous about leaving the kids for the night. With a blue uniform at the house I was pretty sure things would be all right on that front. Later that evening we went to a small restaurant in the heart of town. We both ordered a chicken salad with blue cheese on the side. As we picked at our salads, I could tell that Sherry was a bit distant; but who wouldn't be after what we had been through.

"Hey kid," I said with a smile, "are you all right?"

"Jake," she said, "have you thought about the long term consequences of your new life. I mean do you know what you doing to your children?"

"Well," I said, "I don't really like it but I know I have been called to do something different. Besides with Ieke out there, none of us is really all that safe."

I received a call from Chris later that evening. "Do you think you can be ready to get back at it in a few days," he asked.

I was silent for a few seconds and then said, "After a great deal of reflection we have decided to leave the kids with their grandparents."

Christian agreed to provide everyone with new identities and a new location.

We found out later that Sam's attacker carried a fake passport and had only been in the country a few days. A preliminary US State Department investigation determined that the attacker may have been from Turkey. He carried a handwritten letter with him that in part stated, "Shabop, Glad you have recovered from your snake bites. Rather than go home to Turkey, I have another job for you. Can you get to Seattle…" Thanks Carlos.

The story Sam's attacker told the police was not believable. He said he had, "seen our pictures in the paper and I thought, might try to extort a little money to get home on."

KNIGHT JUSTICE

"Clearly he is a nut." The officer said as he finished briefing me on the status of the situation.

I was not so sure, I was pretty confident that Rollands was behind this half-baked scheme. I discussed what I knew with Chris. I was careful not to give him a great deal of my personal feelings but I carefuliy tried to provide only the facts. I let him know that I was not too happy about the investigation on Ieke but I was left to wait until I had something to go on. Now Sherry and I were off to who knows where and my entire family was off to someplace in Arizona. My parents and the kids ended up in a little town in Arizona called Prescott and we had been informed that Sherry and I were flying out to DC. I had just a few days to get things in order.

CHAPTER 40

Six Months Later, Old Beginnings

As Sherry and I walked along the Fashion Square Mall In Scottsdale, Arizona I showed her the Seattle Star headline. It read, "Castilano convicted." The paper said he was guilty of criminal trespass, felony theft and conspiracy."

I had to finish the entire article and as I noticed a nice bench, I asked Sherry to have a seat. I walked over and purchased a couple of Seabucks ice coffees at the stand across the walkway. We sat on the bench below the escalators reading the paper and sipping our creamy cool coffee. It was not too bitter.

On the front page of the article it also said, "Kareem Razier, a former local teacher was convicted of kidnapping and given a 10 year sentence."

He got off easy with one year in prison and the remainder on probation as part of a plea bargain deal.

"Other trials are still pending."

Then I read the kicker.

"The big fish is still at large. Ieke Rollands, former Seattle schools superintendent is still at large, assumed to be somewhere in Central or South America according to unnamed sources."

"Wow," I said to Sherry as she smiled back, "what a ride this has been." Acting like I was going to toss the paper, I walked over to a waste basket. It was at the end of the bench. I bent down on one knee and picked up a small black box. I looked up at Sherry with a one sided smile and said, "Look what I found."

I saw her eyes widen.

I said, "Sherry Paul will you marry me?"

Sherry laughed and said, "Only if you take me on a new adventure that does not involve any caves."

I said, "I don't recall many caves in Central America." We both laughed as she put the one carat diamond on her finger.

The next morning, I received a call from Chris. "Pack your bags, you and Sherry are to be in DC on Monday. Your flight information is in your email." He hung up.

As we drove to the airport Sherry turned and said, "I guess our pending marriage will have to wait huh."

"I guess." I said.

We boarded the plane and took off on schedule. When we arrived at Reagan National, The Old Man was there to greet us. We drove the short distance to Christian's office.

As we walked in Chris started, "Dearly beloved we are gathered here…"

A few minutes later we were married. Chris handed me a packet. He said, "Congratulations you two, the Old Man will take you back to the airport your instructions are in your packet." Sherry just looked at me and smiled.

I looked at her as if to say was I just set up again? I turned and followed the Old Man back to the car. Less than an hour later we were on a plane headed to Munich Germany. We landed at the airport where a Sigma Knight picked us up. Sherry handed him a document which contained computer codes and specific instructions. Sherry spent about twenty minutes going over the document and answering questions. She reminded him that he was now in the possession of the only copy of the fix she proposed. He grabbed the document, grunted a few times and walked away.

"When did you have time to work on that," I asked.

Sherry smiled and said, "Jake what do you think I was doing while you were sleeping on the plane? Can you think of a more secure location than thirty thousand feet in the air?"

To that we both had a laugh. The shuttle trip from the airport was quite short. It was 9:00 PM when we arrived at the small inn just outside Werfen Austria. The older lady at the front desk looked at us with not so much as a grin.

"You vill be here one night, yah." She said with a thick accent. I nodded affirmatively. It was late and we were tired. The rustic inn was finished in pine and was quite small. We were escorted to our room which was no larger than ten feet by ten feet square. There were two small twin beds. Each was covered with a down blanket.

I looked at Sherry and said, "good night my bride."

She smiled demurely, eyes half closed with exhaustion and replied, Goodnight my Prince."

We crawled into our separate beds and feel asleep.

The next morning we were awakened by a knock at the door. It was room service. Believe it or not this small inn located on the outskirts of Werfen provided room service. We enjoyed fresh squeezed orange juice and eggs with melon and grapes. By 9:30 AM we about ready to take on the day. We were a bit groggy from the jet lag. I walked over to the window and opened the curtains.

A little extra sun might help.

I yelled at Sherry, "Hey sweetie you have got to see this."

Sherry walked out of the tiny bathroom and looked out over the pastoral valley. There, across the river, partially shrouded in clouds was one of the most beautiful sites I had ever seen. Sherry was frozen.

Then all of a sudden, she swung open the little door and popped out onto the deck just outside the room. I was a step behind her. There on the top of a mountain just a few hundred yards from our room was a Castle. The clouds flowed slowly over the site giving it an almost animated appearance. I was transfixed by its beauty. Finally I looked over at Sherry and tears were streaming down her face.

She turned to me, hugged me tightly and said, "Jake there is nobody on this planet I would rather share this with and there is no place I would rather be than right here with you."

I moved my head slowly towards hers as she moved in on me. Our lips met and the chemistry was supercharged. As we kissed, it seemed we were spinning into each other. Slowly at first and then we fell into a mixed up swirl of emotion. We kissed for what must have been a multitude of minutes. It was wonderful.

⚔

Later that morning we walked down through the Salzach Valley. We marveled at the Berchtesgaden Alps and Tennengebrige mountains that seemed to dwarf the Hohenwerfen Castle.

As we strolled along the trail following the Salzach River, Sherry said, "Jake this is where our new adventure begins. After dinner we headed to the giant ice world where we were to be driven to a special spot. I can't wait, isn't this valley and this location beautiful Jake?"

"Indescribable," I said with a grin.

We spent the evening at a small restaurant in the Hotel Hochthorn in Werfenweng in the hills just a few miles outside Werfen. Sherry ordered pfeferlinges. These wild mushrooms were cooked just right. I ate roulade which is like a big steak and for dessert we enjoyed preiselbeeran a great berry pie. It was rustic and homey. Just the feeling we wanted. After dinner we watched the sun slowly set over the Alps. I was in heaven. Sherry was growing stronger and happier by the minute.

I was happy to be there with Sherry and I wanted to know if she was as taken with the beauty of the place as I was.

After a number of false starts, as we were sharing a small dish of ice cream, I finally turned to Sherry, looked her in the eye and said, "Do you remember when this adventure began?"

Sherry got up from her seat put her arms around me, and replied, "The cabin on the island; this feels the same."

I really didn't mind that the only other couple in the room was gawking at us. Following dinner we hiked the short distance to the waiting 1963 Grand Sport Racing Corvette that was left for us. It had an all–aluminum 377-CID smallblock V-8. It only generated about 550 horsepower. It was one of five produced. Needless to say it was a sweet ride. It was like a 1963 stingray but a lot faster. It purred like a kitten, well, really more like a lion. I drove to the entrance of the Ice caves where we were met by our guide. We got into a small car that resembled an ice cat. As I recall it had six rubber tires outfitted with snow tracks. It was a cool little machine.

"Do you see the crystal ice tunnels?" The driver said, as we were whisked through the sparkling fantasyland.

Sherry said, "Jake can you see the ice crystals, they sparkle in the cold summer air? They are like pixie dust."

How can we miss them, they surround us, I thought as we slowly made our way deeper into the darkening tunnel.

An hour later we arrived outside Berchtesgaden on the German Austrian border. We transferred to a van. We were treated to a stomach churning drive up a road filled with hairpin turns. It was cold and dark. After about a half hour, the driver stopped the car. We were in a large parking lot. It looked like some tourist location.

The driver said, "Walk across the lot and follow the paved path. You will see a tunnel. Follow the walkway to the end."

I picked up both suit cases and Sherry grabbed the packet Chris had given us. We were on our way to somewhere. I was not sure exactly where. I was sure it couldn't top what we had already seen today. We headed up the dark tunnel. When we reached the end of the tunnel there was a large circular room, on one side was an elevator where an attendant was standing in the open door. I swear it looked like a scene from some 1940's vintage horror movie. It was not so much the looks because the granite and tile were striking. It was the thought of it all. We were standing where Hitler and other Nazi murderers stood some 50 years earlier. To me that was unnerving.

We got into the elevator anyway. As we stood in the elevator I noticed how large and beautiful it really was. The interior was appointed in polished brass finished off with green leather as a wainscot. There were also beautiful Venetian mirrors trimmed in brass. The operator took us to the tenth floor. That was weird because I noticed on the floor indicator the top floor said Eagle's Nest. The Eagles Nest was many floors above where we were stopped.

I pointed to the words eagles nest and asked, "Is this The Eagles Nest, Hitler's lair?" He looked at me, smiled and nodded affirmatively.

When the doors opened, the attendant said, "Enjoy your Honeymoon."

While I was a bit wary, I was pretty sure Chris would not treat us badly. Not on this day. So I smiled and grabbed Sherry in a two armed squeeze. We spun around three times. The operator did not crack as much as a smile. The doors of the beautiful old elevator slid open. As they did, I wondered how much different it must have been for the members of the third Reich when they used it exclusively for Hitler and his friends. Of course, at that time, the Eagles Nest, Hitler's World War II hideaway was the primary destination. What I did not know, until that moment, was that the top floor, where the hideaway is, is only one of many stops. Some floors now belong to the United States CIA and the British Interpol and certain other groups.

"The street car is waiting outside," the attendant announced.

Sherry said, "Have you ever seen such a shiny little red wagon. The tracks are so small."

I turned to Sherry and said, "This looks more like a Disneyland trolley to me then a street car."

"Where are your lederhosen?" Sherry joked.

I turned back as the doors slowly closed and I noticed, etched into the stone next to the doors were the words "Kilroy was here."

That was almost expected, but over those words, the words "Ieke is watching you," were written in chalk. That was not expected or humorous. I quickly grabbed Sherry by the arm and squired her into the car. I hoped she had not seen what I had. What Sherry and I soon discovered, was that the salt mines under much of Austria and parts of Germany were connected via caves and tunnels to Salzburg and many cities including Brechtesgaden. We had already experienced part of the system which included the Ice Caves.

The little electric shuttle moved along at around twenty miles per hour. We moved through miles of tunnels. As we traveled along, almost entirely underground, I noticed most of the walls were dimly lit. From time to time we moved into large rooms, better described as warehouses or museums. Certain of these rooms contained art work and treasures of unmatched beauty. We stopped the car and got out. I noticed paintings by Leonardo Da Vinci. One especially caught my eye.

It was the finished painting of "The Adoration of the Magi." It was done in vibrant reds, whites and brilliant purples and the gold of the manger seemed to radiate off the canvas. Can you imagine what people would do if they knew there were hundreds of previously unknown pieces of art produced by the masters. It was as if we were on a private tour of lost art treasures. Magnificent works by Michelangelo I had never heard of were also there.

Brilliant marble busts of children at play caught Sherry's eye. "Jake did you know that these are the works that disappeared during the Nazi occupation? These works were not registered or recorded by the allies or the Nazis."

Sherry sat transfixed by the splendor of it all. "I wonder if the temperature, humidity and salt in the caves is helpful in preserving the treasures?" She asked.

Sherry said, "When the allies defeated Germany in World War II the confiscated art was recovered from the Nazis. There were many treasures. Most were returned to their original owners."

I said, "well apparently not all of them were returned to the owner's right?"

Sherry said, "We will be dealing with this matter shortly but for now let's just enjoy the view."

After what seemed like minutes we climbed back on the car. We were off again. I cannot tell you with any degree of accuracy, the beauty contained in the underground tunnels we saw on the ride through the salt caves. At a certain point as the cable car moved along we passed a long section of tracks that sparkled in the dim light. It was the white salt that was catching the light. It was entrancing.

Sherry said, "The Knights of St. John have been accessing these tunnels since the middle ages and in fact our group was given access to certain of these tunnels that connected castles and chambers as part of the meeting that gave rise to the 1805 Treaty of Pressburg."

Anyway, the street car took us to a backdoor entrance to a penthouse suite built within a basement section of the old Castle, "Festung Hohensalzburg". We got off the elevator. It opened into a beautiful suite. Sherry took the letter from Chris that was given us when we left DC and tossed it on the bed.

Then she ran over, jumped on the bed and opened the letter that was in the packet Chris had given us.

Chuckling she began to Read:

Sherry did you get your work done? If so congratulations, you have earned a well-deserved honeymoon. Enjoy the sights and sounds of Austria. The Knights are at your disposal twentyfour hours a day. Make sure you enjoy the street cars. You are two of only a few thousand people in the world who know they exist. I didn't say it but you heard it. I expect by now you will have enjoyed your travels through the salt caves. Did you like the ice caves? By the way, check out St. Wolfgang's sea while you are there. I think the two of you can use a little music in your life. See you in a few weeks. We have a lot of work to do when you return!
Sincerely,
Christian

Sherry looked at me with a wide smile and said, "I thought I told you no more caves."

Made in the USA
San Bernardino, CA
25 June 2017